BETSY AND TACY GO
OVER THE BIG HILL

Betsy and Tacy Go Over the Big Hill

by

Maud Hart Lovelace

Illustrated

by

Lois Lenski

■■ HarperCollins*Publishers*

First published by Thomas Y. Crowell Company in 1942.
Library of Congress Catalog Card Number 42-23557
ISBN 0-690-13521-1 (lib. bdg.)
ISBN 0-06-440099-9 (pbk.)

FOR

KATHLEEN AND TESS,

the villains of the piece

CONTENTS

Hills were higher then

—HUGH MAC NAIR KAHLER

I

GETTING TO BE TEN

BETSY, Tacy, and Tib were nine years old, and they were very anxious to be ten.

"You have two numbers in your age when you are ten. It's the beginning of growing up," Betsy would say.

Then the three of them felt solemn and important and pleased. They could hardly wait for their birthdays.

It was strange that Betsy and Tacy and Tib were in such a hurry to grow up, for they had so much fun being children. Betsy and Tacy lived on Hill Street which ran straight up into a green hill and stopped. The small yellow cottage where Betsy Ray lived was the last house on that side of the street, and the rambling white house opposite where Tacy Kelly lived was the last house on that side. They had the whole hill for a playground. And not just that one green slope. There were hills all around them. Hills like a half-opened fan rose in the east behind Betsy's house. Beyond the town and across the river where the sun set there were more hills. The name of the town was Deep Valley.

Tib didn't live on Hill Street. To get to Tib's house from the place where Betsy and Tacy lived, you went one block down and one block over. (The second block was through a vacant lot.) But Tib lived near enough to come to play with Betsy and Tacy. She came every day.

"They certainly have fun, those three," Betsy's mother used to say to Betsy's father.

They did, too.

Betsy's big sister Julia played with Tacy's sister

2

Katie, but they didn't have so much fun as Betsy and Tacy and Tib had. They were too grown up. They were twelve.

Betsy's little sister Margaret, Tacy's younger brother Paul, and Tib's yellow-headed brothers, Freddie and Hobbie, had fun all right, but not so much fun as Betsy and Tacy and Tib had. They were too little.

Going on ten seemed to be exactly the right age for having fun. But just the same Betsy and Tacy and Tib wanted to be ten years old.

They were getting near it now. Betsy and Tacy were growing tall, so that their mothers were kept busy lengthening their dresses. Tib wasn't as tiny as she used to be, but she was still tiny. She still looked like a picture-book fairy. The three girls had cut their hair when they were eight years old and didn't know any better, but it had grown out. Tib's curls once more made a yellow fluff around her little face. Tacy had her long red ringlets and Betsy had her braids again.

"When I'm ten," said Betsy, "I'm going to cross my braids in back and tie them with ribbons."

"I'm going to tie my hair at my neck with a big blue bow," Tacy replied.

"We can't put it up in pugs *quite* yet, I suppose," Betsy said.

"But pretty soon we can," said Tacy. "On top of

our heads."

Tib did not make plans like that. She never did.

"I only hope," she said, "that when I get to be ten years old people will stop taking me for a baby."

For people always thought that Tib was younger than she was. And she didn't like it a bit.

Tacy got to be ten first because her birthday came in January. They didn't have many birthday parties at Tacy's house. There were too many children in the family. Mrs. Kelly would have been giving birthday parties every month in the year, almost, if every child at the Kelly house had had a party every birthday. But when Tacy was ten, Betsy and Tib were invited to supper. There was a cake with candles on it.

Tacy didn't look any different or feel any different. But she knew why that was. Betsy and Tib weren't ten yet.

"We'll all have to get to be ten before it really counts, I suppose," Tacy said.

Tib got to be ten next because her birthday came in March. Tib didn't have a birthday party; she had the grippe instead. But she was given a bicycle, and her mother sent pieces of birthday cake over to Betsy and Tacy.

And Tib didn't look any different or feel any different. But she didn't expect much change until Betsy got to be ten. And Betsy's birthday didn't come until April.

Tacy and Tib didn't say very much about being ten. They were too polite. They talked about presents and birthday cakes, but they didn't mention having two numbers in their age. They didn't talk about beginning to grow up until the afternoon before Betsy's birthday.

That afternoon after school they all went up on the Big Hill hunting for violets. It was one of those April days on which it seemed that summer had already come, although the ground was still muddy and brown. The sun was shining so warmly that Betsy, Tacy, and Tib pulled off their stocking caps and unbuttoned their coats. Birds in the bare trees

5

were singing with all their might, and Betsy, Tacy, and Tib sang too as they climbed the Big Hill.

They sang to the tune of "Mine eyes have seen the glory," but they made up the words themselves:

> "Oh, Betsy's ten tomorrow,
> And then all of us are ten,
> We will all grow up tomorrow,
> We will all be ladies then. . . ."

They marched in a row and sang.

The Ekstroms, whose white house stood at the top of the hill, were out making garden. It made them laugh to see Betsy, Tacy, and Tib marching along and singing. Betsy, Tacy, and Tib liked to make the Ekstroms laugh. They marched straighter and sang louder than ever.

Marching and singing, they turned to the right and went through the twin row of beeches which they called their Secret Lane, and past the foundations of that house which had never been finished which they called the Mystery House. Still marching and singing, they went down through a fold of the hills and up again. But now they had sung until they were hoarse, and they burst out laughing and fell down on top of each other.

When they were rested Tib stood up.

"We'd better get those violets," she said.

But Tacy cried out, "Look! We've come farther than we ever came before."

Sure enough, they stood on a part of the hill which was new to them. Climbing a little higher, they left the trees behind and came out on a high rocky ridge. Below, spread out in the sunlight, was a strange wide beautiful valley. In the center were one big brick house and a row of tiny houses.

"That looks like Little Syria," said Tib.

"It can't be!" cried Betsy and Tacy together, for Little Syria was a place they went to with their fathers and mothers when out buggy riding on a summer evening. It was not a place one saw when one went walking.

Yet this was certainly Little Syria.

"That big brick house is the Meecham Mansion," Tib said.

It certainly was.

Mr. Meecham had built it many years before, according to the story which Betsy and Tacy and Tib had often heard their fathers tell. He had come from the East and had bought all the land in this valley, calling it Meecham's Addition. He had tried to sell lots there, but none of his American neighbors had wished to live so far from the center of town. At last he had sold his lots to a colony of Syrians, strange dark people who spoke broken English and came to Hill Street sometimes peddling garden stuff and laces and embroidered cloths.

Angry and disappointed, Mr. Meecham lived on in his mansion among the humble houses of the Syrians. So did his wife until she died. And so did his middle-aged daughter. He was a tall old man with a flowing white beard and a proud scornful bearing. His team of white horses was the finest in the county; and it was driven by a coachman. Mr. Meecham and his daughter came to town in style, when they came, which was not often.

Little Syria belonged to Deep Valley but it seemed

as foreign as though it were across the ocean.

And now here it lay, at the very feet of Betsy, Tacy, and Tib.

The three of them stared down at it, and Betsy was thinking hard.

"Well, I'm surprised!" said Tacy. "I never knew we could walk to Little Syria."

"I'm not surprised," said Betsy.

"You're not?" asked Tacy.

"No," said Betsy. "Remember I'll be ten tomorrow. It's the sort of thing we'll be doing often from now on."

"Going to other towns?" asked Tacy.

"Yes. Little Syria. Minneapolis. Chicago. New York."

"I'd love to go to New York and see the Flatiron Building," said Tacy.

Tib looked puzzled.

"But Little Syria," she said, "is just over our own hill. We didn't know that it was. But it is."

"Well, we certainly didn't find it out until today," said Betsy.

"We certainly never walked to it before," said Tacy.

"That's right," admitted Tib.

They gazed down on Little Syria in the center of the broad calm valley. Mr. Meecham's Mansion with the little houses in a row looked like a hen followed by chicks.

"Shall we go down?" asked Tib, dancing about. Tib liked to do things instead of talking about them.

It was a daring suggestion. There were tales of the Syrians fighting one another with knives. A man called Old Bushara had once chased a boy with a knife. The boy was in their grade at school.

"Remember Sam and Old Bushara?" Tacy asked now.

"Sam's a horrid boy," said Tib. "He yelled 'dago' at Old Bushara. He yells that at all the Syrians and it's not a nice thing to do. Shall we go down?" she persisted, hopping from foot to foot.

Betsy looked at Tacy.

"Not today," she said. "It's too late. But some day we'll go."

They walked back slowly, picking flowers as they went. They didn't find many violets, but they found bloodroots, and Dutchman's breeches, and hepaticas, rising from the damp brown mat which carpeted the ground. They didn't march or sing going home. When they passed the Ekstroms' house, the Ekstroms, who were making a bonfire now, called out to ask where the parade was.

"What parade?" asked Betsy. "Oh, that! We won't be parading much more, I expect."

"Betsy will be ten years old tomorrow, Mrs. Ekstrom," Tacy said.

"And then we'll all be ten," said Tib.

"You don't say!" Mrs. Ekstrom answered.

They started down the hill.

Before they were halfway down, the sun hid itself behind purple curtains. And the air which had been so summerlike grew suddenly remindful of winter. Betsy, Tacy, and Tib pulled on their stocking caps and buttoned their flapping coats.

"That was our last parade, I expect," said Betsy.

"Why?" asked Tib. "I think they're fun."

"We're getting too old for them," Tacy said.

"That's right," said Betsy. "Marching along and yelling will seem pretty childish after tomorrow."

"I suppose we'll start having tea parties," said Tacy.

"Yes. We'll crook our little fingers over the cups like *this*," answered Betsy, crooking her little finger in a very elegant way.

"We'll say 'indeed' to each other," said Tacy.

"And 'prefer,' " said Betsy.

"Will it be fun?" asked Tib. She sounded as though she didn't think it would be.

"Fun or not," said Betsy, "we have to grow up. Everyone does."

"And we're beginning tomorrow," said Tacy. "On

Betsy's birthday."

They had reached Betsy's hitching block and Betsy wished she could say something more about her birthday. She wished she could invite Tacy and Tib to her birthday supper. But her mother hadn't said a word about inviting them. In fact, her mother did not seem to take much interest in this birthday. Betsy wondered if that was because she was growing up.

"See you tomorrow," she said, because there was nothing better to say, and she waved good-by and ran into the house. For the first time she had a queer feeling inside about getting to be ten years old.

She woke up in the night and had the feeling again. She lay very still in the bed she shared with Julia and thought about growing up. The window at the front of the little tent-roofed bedroom which looked across to Tacy's house showed squares of dismal gray.

"Maybe it's not so nice growing up. Maybe it's more fun being a child," thought Betsy. "Well, anyway, there's nothing I can do about it!"

She dropped off to sleep.

And next morning when she woke up she was ten years old.

Betsy, Tacy, and Tib were ten years old at last.

II

TEN YEARS OLD

IN THE morning it seemed thrilling to be ten years old.

Betsy jumped out of bed and ran to the window. The lawn, the road, the branches of the trees, and Tacy's roof across the street were skimmed with snow. But she knew it could not last, in April.

"Happy birthday!" said Julia, struggling into her underwear beside the warm chimney which angled up from the hard coal heater downstairs. She spoke politely. She did not pound Betsy on the back as on other birthday mornings. But Betsy suspected that Julia was thinking more of the dignity of her own twelve years than of Betsy's ten.

Betsy answered carelessly, "That's right. It *is* my birthday."

She dressed and went humming carelessly down the stairs.

Her father pounded her plenty. And he held her while Margaret pounded. She was pounded and tickled and kissed. Of course it was hard to act careless during such a rumpus, but after it was over Betsy acted careless again. She crooked her finger when she lifted her milk glass, but just a little; she was afraid that Julia would notice.

"Don't you feel well, Betsy?" asked her mother.

"Why, yes," said Betsy. "I feel fine."

"She's very quiet," said her father. "It's the weight of her years."

Betsy was startled until she saw that her father was joking. Her father was a great one to joke.

The pounding and joking showed that her birthday was remembered but still nobody mentioned asking Tacy and Tib to supper. Betsy got ready for school slowly. When her father left for the shoe store, she was still dawdling over her coat and stocking cap, tangling her mitten strings, and losing her rubbers. She gave her mother plenty of chance to bring up the subject. But it didn't do any good.

At last Betsy said, "Hadn't I better ask Tacy and Tib over to supper, mamma?"

"Not today," answered Mrs. Ray. She sounded for all the world as though any other day would do as well.

"Mamma's pretty busy today. You know Friday's cleaning day," Julia said importantly.

Cleaning day! Betsy could hardly believe her ears.

She tried to act as though it didn't matter.

"When I was only nine I would have teased," she thought.

She kissed her mother good-by and went humming out the door and across the street to Tacy's.

Mrs. Kelly came to the door and said, "Isn't this your birthday, Betsy?"

"*Indeed* it is," said Betsy, stressing the "indeed" and looking hard at Tacy. Her manner was light and careless, very grown-up.

Mrs. Kelly did not seem to notice the grown-upness. She took Betsy's round red cheeks in her hands and said, "It's five years today that you and

Tacy have been friends."

"Goodness!" said Betsy, forgetting to act old for a minute because she *felt* so old.

But she and Tacy acted old all the way down Hill Street, and even more so after they had cut through the vacant lot to Pleasant Street and called for Tib at her beautiful chocolate-colored house. It was fun to watch Tib's round blue eyes grow rounder as she listened to them talk.

"Will you both come to tea some day this week?" Betsy asked carelessly.

"Yes *indeed*," said Tacy. "I'd love to. Wouldn't you, Tib?"

"Um-hum," said Tib.

"When I get some money," said Betsy, "I'm going to buy some nail powder. I'm going to start buffing my nails. I think we all ought to."

"So do I," said Tacy. "I think my sister Mary would lend us a little nail powder, maybe."

"Do you really?" asked Betsy.

"Yes *indeed*," said Tacy. Tacy loved to say "indeed."

Tib didn't know how to talk in the new way. She hadn't learned yet. But she tried.

"I borrowed my mamma's nail powder once and I spilled it," she said.

Betsy and Tacy hurried over that.

"We must buy some hair pins too," said Betsy. "Of course we're not quite ready to put up our hair, but we shall be soon."

"I can hardly wait to get my skirts down," Tacy said. "Ankle length is what I prefer."

"What do you prefer, Tib?" asked Betsy.

"I don't know what 'prefer' means, exactly," said Tib. "Betsy, do you think I still look like a baby?"

Betsy glanced at her and hastily glanced away.

"Not so much as you did yesterday," she said.

"Try to talk like us, Tib," Tacy advised. "It's easy when you get started."

They talked grown-up all the way to school; and they kept on doing it coming home from school at noon, and going back after dinner, and coming home again at three o'clock.

On that trip, when they reached the corner by Tib's house, Betsy felt a strong return of that queer feeling inside. The snow was melting and the ground was slushy and damp. It wasn't a good time for playing out. Today of all days, she should be asking Tacy and Tib to come to her house. And her mother had told her not to!

Tacy and Tib acted embarrassed. Tacy looked at Tib and Tib looked at Tacy and said, "Why don't you come into my house to play?"

"I'd like to. Wouldn't you, Betsy?" Tacy asked.

"There are some funny papers you haven't seen," said Tib. "Is it all right for us to look at them, now we are ten?"

"Of course," said Tacy hastily. "Lots of grown people read the funny papers. Don't they, Betsy?"

"Oh, of course!" Betsy said.

So they went into Tib's house where they always loved to go; it was so beautiful with a tower on the front and panes of colored glass in the front door. They sat on the window seat and looked at the funny

papers, crooking their fingers when they turned the pages. Betsy began to feel better. She had an idea.

"I think we're too old," she said, "to call each other by our nicknames any more. I think we ought to start using our real names. For instance, you should call me Elizabeth."

"Yes," said Tacy. "And you should call me Anastacia."

"And you should call me Thelma," said Tib. "Hello, Anastacia! How-de-do, Elizabeth?"

The big names made them laugh. Whenever they said "Anastacia" they laughed so hard that they rolled on the window seat.

Matilda, the hired girl, came in from the kitchen.

"What's going on in here?" she asked, looking cross. Matilda almost always looked cross.

"Anastacia and Elizabeth are making me laugh," said Tib.

"No. It's Thelma acting silly," cried Betsy and Tacy.

"Where are all those folks?" asked Matilda, looking around. Betsy, Tacy, and Tib shouted at that.

They had such a good time that Betsy almost forgot how strange it was not to have Tacy and Tib come to supper on her most important birthday. But when the time came to go home she remembered.

"Tacy," she said, as they walked through the vacant

lot, "people don't make as much fuss about birthdays after other people grow up. Have you noticed that?"

"Um—er," said Tacy. She acted embarrassed again.

"Not that it matters, of course," said Betsy. "It doesn't matter a bit."

It did, though.

It was dusk when she reached home but no lamps had been lighted except in the kitchen where Mrs. Ray was bustling about getting supper. She wore a brown velvet bow in her high red pompadour and a fresh brown checked apron tied around her slender waist.

Julia was scrubbing Margaret at the basin. And Julia too looked very spic and span.

"Clean up good for supper, Betsy," her mother said.

"Yes, ma'am," said Betsy.

"Mamma," said Julia, "don't you think Betsy ought to put on her new plaid hair ribbons?"

"Yes, that's a good idea," said Mrs. Ray.

"After all, it's her birthday," said Julia, and Margaret clapped her wet hand over her mouth and said, "Oh! Oh!" Margaret was only four years old.

"Probably she thinks Julia is giving something away. Probably she thinks I don't know we'll have a

birthday cake," thought Betsy. And then she thought, "Maybe we won't. Things get so different as you get older." She felt gloomy.

But she scrubbed her face and hands. And Julia helped her braid her hair and even crossed the braids in back; they were just long enough to cross. Julia tied the plaid bows perkily over Betsy's ears.

When she was cleaned up, Betsy went into the back parlor. The fire was shining through the isinglass windows of the hard coal heater there. It looked cozy and she would have enjoyed sitting down beside it with a book. But her mother called out:

"Betsy, I borrowed an egg today from Mrs. Rivers. Will you return it for me, please?"

"Right now?" asked Betsy.

"Yes, please," her mother answered.

"Of all things!" said Betsy to herself.

It seemed to her that she might return the egg tomorrow. It seemed to her that Julia might do the errands on this particular day. It was a nuisance getting into outdoor clothes when she had just taken them off.

"What must I wear?" she asked, trying not to show she was cross because it was her birthday.

"You'll only need your coat and rubbers. Go out the back way," her mother said.

So Betsy put on her coat and rubbers and took an egg and went out the back way.

Mrs. Rivers lived next door, and she was very nice. She had a little girl just Margaret's age, and a still smaller girl, and a baby. The baby was sitting in a high chair eating his supper and Mrs. Rivers asked Betsy to stay a moment and watch him. He was just learning how to feed himself and he was funny.

Betsy stayed and watched him. And she said "indeed" and "prefer" to Mrs. Rivers and that cheered her up a little. Mrs. Rivers kept looking out of the window. At last she said:

"I'm afraid your mother will be expecting you

now. Good-by, dear. Go out the back way."

So Betsy went out the back way and climbed the little slope which led to her house. The ground was slippery, for the melted snow had frozen again. The stars above the hill were icy white.

She went into the house dejectedly. There was no one in the kitchen. The door which led to the dining room was closed.

"They've started supper without me. On my birth-day!" Betsy thought. She felt like sitting down and crying.

She opened the dining room door and then stopped. No wonder she stopped! The room was crowded with children. They called, "Surprise! Surprise! Surprise on Betsy!"

Betsy's father stood there with his arm around Betsy's mother and both of them were smiling. Tacy and Tib rushed over to Betsy and began to pound her on the back, and Julia ran into the front parlor and started playing the piano. Everybody sang:

> "Happy birthday to you!
> Happy birthday to you!
> Happy birthday, dear Betsy,
> Happy birthday to you!"

"It's a surprise party," cried Margaret, red-faced from joyful suspense.

It was certainly a surprise.

There were ten little girls at the party because Betsy was ten years old. Ten little girls, that is, without Margaret who was too little to count. Betsy made one, and Julia made two, and Tacy made three, and Katie made four, and Tib made five, and a little girl named Alice who lived down on Pleasant Street made six, and Julia's and Katie's friend Dorothy who also lived down on Pleasant Street made seven, and three little girls from Betsy's class in school made eight, nine, and ten.

There were ten candles on the birthday cake, but before they had the birthday cake they had sandwiches and cocoa: and along with the birthday cake they had ice cream; and after the birthday cake they played games in the front and back parlors. Betsy's father played with them; Betsy's mother played the piano for Going to Jerusalem; and when Betsy's father was left without a chair how everybody laughed!

Betsy and Tacy and Tib played harder than anyone. They forgot to crook their fingers and to say "indeed" and "prefer." They forgot to call one another Elizabeth and Anastacia and Thelma. In fact, after that day, they never did these things again.

But just the same, in the midst of the excitement, Betsy realized that she was practically grown up.

Flushed and panting from Blind Man's Buff, her

braids loose, and her best hair ribbons untied, she found her mother.

"Mamma," she said, "this is the first party I ever had at night."

"That's right," her mother answered. "The children are staying until nine o'clock, and papa is taking them home."

"Is it because I'm ten years old?" asked Betsy.

"Of course it is," her mother answered.

Betsy rushed to find Tacy and Tib. She drew them into a corner.

"You notice," she whispered proudly, "that we're having this party at night."

"What about it?" asked Tib.

"What about it?" repeated Betsy. "Why, it's a grown-up party."

"It's practically a ball," said Tacy.

"Oh," said Tib.

"Of course," she pointed out after a moment, "tomorrow isn't a school day."

Tib always mentioned things like that. But Betsy and Tacy liked her just the same.

III

THE KING OF SPAIN

THE first thing Betsy and Tacy and Tib did after they were ten years old was to fall in love. They all fell in love at once . . . with the same person too.

It happened this way.

Betsy was eating her supper. She was hurrying in order to get out to play, for on May evenings all the children of Hill Street gathered in the street to play. They played Run-Sheep-Run and Prisoners' Base and Pom-Pom-Pullaway and many other games, until the sun finally set behind Tacy's house and the first stars appeared in the sky. Betsy loved this wild hour of play and she usually thought about it all through supper, but tonight her attention was caught by something her father was saying.

"Sixteen years old. It's pretty young to be a king."

"Has he had his birthday yet?" Betsy's mother asked.

"Not yet. But they're making great preparations. You see, he comes to the throne that day." Mr. Ray folded the paper and handed it to his wife. "There's his picture. Handsome boy, isn't he?"

Julia and Betsy jumped up and looked over their mother's shoulder. They saw the picture of a slim dark boy on horseback. The line beneath the picture read:

"Alphonso the Thirteenth."

"Do you mean he's living some place? Right now?" asked Betsy.

"Yes," her mother answered. "He lives in Spain."

"That country we had the war with," said Julia. "It's your turn to wipe the dishes, Betsy."

"It is not," said Betsy. "I wiped them last night."

"But that was making up for the night before, when I did them for you, while you and Tacy practiced the 'Cat Duet.' "

Betsy could not deny it.

"And tonight," said Julia, "I have to practice my recitation."

There was lots of practicing going on, for there was to be a big Entertainment on the Last Day of School.

"All right," said Betsy. She didn't mind staying in to wipe dishes as much as usual. It was a chance to ask her mother about the King of Spain.

She had known, of course, that there were kings and queens outside of fairy tales and histories. But she had never thought much about them before. It was strange to think now of a real live boy being a king.

She listened eagerly while her mother told her all she knew about him.

His father had died many years before; his mother, the Queen, had been acting as regent; but on May seventeenth he would be sixteen years old, and then he would ascend the throne and rule the country himself.

"Madrid . . . that's the capital of Spain . . . is turned inside out with excitement," Betsy's mother said.

Betsy felt turned inside out with excitement too. After the towels had been hung to dry, she ran into the back parlor to find the newspaper. Fortunately her father had finished with it; he had gone to work in the garden. Clutching the paper, Betsy ran outdoors.

Games had begun but Tacy was not playing. She was sitting on the hitching block waiting for Betsy. The sun was low and the new leaves on the trees shimmered in a golden light.

"Tacy!" cried Betsy. "Did you know there was a king in Europe . . . alive and everything . . . only fifteen years old?"

"I've heard about him," Tacy said.

"Here's a picture of him," said Betsy. She sat down beside Tacy on the hitching block and they looked at the picture together.

"Just think!" said Betsy. "We're sitting here on the hitching block and at this very minute he's *somewhere, doing something.*"

"Maybe he's eating his supper," Tacy said.

"Maybe he's out horseback riding, like he was when this picture was taken."

"Maybe he's saying his prayers."

"Maybe he's blowing his nose."

"It seems queer to have him blowing his nose,"

said Tacy, looking displeased.

"Oh, probably he has an embroidered handker-chief," said Betsy. "I imagine he does."

They looked at the picture again.

"Tacy," said Betsy. "Do you know what?"

"What?" asked Tacy.

"I'm in love with him," said Betsy. "It's the first time I've ever been in love."

"Do you want to marry him?" asked Tacy.

"Yes," said Betsy. "I do. Do you?"

"I certainly do," Tacy said.

The games on the street were going full swing now, but neither Betsy nor Tacy cared about joining in. They sat looking at the King of Spain's picture which was gilded by the sunset light.

Just then Tib ran up, breathless.

"My mamma . . ." she began.

"Tib," said Betsy, interrupting. "Did you know there was a king in Europe, not sixteen years old yet?"

"Is there?" asked Tib.

"Here's his picture," said Tacy. "Betsy and I are in love with him."

"We want to marry him," said Betsy. "We'll be queen if we do."

"Could you both be queen?" asked Tib, staring.

"No, just one of us," said Betsy. "And it had better be Tacy because of her ringlets. She'd look nice in a

crown."

"Tib would make a nice queen," said Tacy. Tacy was shy. She didn't like the idea of being a queen very well.

"My mamma," said Tib, "is making me a white accordion-pleated dress. For the Entertainment. To dance my Baby Dance in. I was hurrying to tell you."

"A white accordion-pleated dress would be fine for a queen," said Tacy. "Don't you think Tib had better be queen, Betsy?"

"If she's in love with him," said Betsy.

Tib could see it was a kind of game.

"If you and Tacy are, I am," she said. "Let's play Pom-Pom-Pullaway now. They're choosing sides."

So they all played Pom-Pom-Pullaway until the golden light on Hill Street changed to soft gray and mothers began calling from the porches. Betsy, Tacy, and Tib didn't talk any more that night about the King of Spain. But they talked about him every night for a long time afterward.

The newspapers were full of news of the young King Alphonso as his sixteenth birthday drew near. Every night when her father had finished with the paper, Betsy took it outdoors. She and Tacy and Tib went up to that bench which stood at the end of Hill Street and there they pored over the printed columns together.

Madrid was a whirlpool of gaiety, they read. The city was planning a Battle of Flowers. The buildings were hung with tapestries and carpets and with red and yellow cloth.

"Red and yellow must be his colors," Betsy remarked thoughtfully.

"We ought to wear them then, like badges," Tacy said. "After all, we're in love with him. We're expecting to marry him. At least, Tib is."

"If we could find some red and yellow cloth, I would make us some badges," Tib said.

Tib could sew.

Betsy and Tacy ran into their houses and rummaged in their mother's scrap bags. Betsy found some red cambric and Tacy found some yellow ribbon, and Tib took these materials home. The next evening she appeared wearing a red and yellow rosette, and when they had climbed the hill to their bench she pinned one on Betsy and one on Tacy. They felt very solemn.

"Now we've got a lodge," said Betsy. "My father belongs to a lodge. It's like a club only more important and very secret."

"Well, this has certainly got to be a secret," Tib said. "Julia and Katie would tease us plenty if they knew we were in love."

"They wouldn't understand being in love with a king," said Betsy. "At least Julia wouldn't. She likes just plain boys. Ordinary boys who walk home from school with her and carry her books, like Ben Williams."

"Katie would think the whole thing was silly," Tacy said.

"That just shows how little she knows about it," said Betsy.

Tib acted embarrassed. She wasn't so much in love as Betsy and Tacy were; she just liked to do whatever they did.

"What is the name of our lodge?" she asked, to change the subject.

"How would K.O.S. be? For King of Spain?" suggested Betsy.

They all thought that was fine.

After that, whenever anyone mentioned "Love" or "Marriage" in their presence, Betsy and Tacy and Tib said "K.O.S." They sighed and rolled their eyes. They wore their red and yellow rosettes faithfully, changing them from one dress to another.

What is more, they wore pictures of the King of Spain, cut from the newspapers, pinned to their underwaists. Betsy had the one in which he sat on a horse. Tacy had one that showed him in hunting costume, with a shawl thrown over one shoulder, a wide hat, and a gun. In Tib's picture he wore a white nautical-looking cap. Betsy and Tacy had a hard time concealing their pictures from Julia and Katie when they undressed at night. That made their secret all the more exciting.

They did not join in the games after dinner any more. Instead they walked up to their bench, and there in the cool spring twilight they read about King Alphonso. His birthday now was drawing very near. In fact, it would come next Saturday.

Peasants, the newspapers said, were flocking into Madrid, wearing the picturesque national costume. Great ladies draped in black lace mantillas sat on balconies.

"What are mantillas?" Tib wanted to know.

"They're shawls," answered Betsy, who had asked her mother.

"I think we ought to have some shawls then," said Tib. "But the only shawl my mamma's got is her old Paisley shawl."

"My mamma's got that heavy brown one we play house with," Betsy said.

"My mamma's got a gray wool one," Tacy said. "She'd let me wear it, I think. We all ought to wear them next Saturday, the day he's crowned."

Betsy and Tib thought so too.

So on Saturday, the seventeenth of May, they wore shawls all day long except at mealtime. It happened that the weather turned very warm that day. The little leaves on the trees seemed to grow bigger by the minute and dandelions on the fresh green lawn almost popped up while you watched them. All up and down Hill Street children put off caps and jackets. But Betsy and Tacy and Tib went around wrapped up in heavy shawls.

The lilacs had come into bloom by Betsy's kitchen door. They picked a bouquet of fragrant purple clusters. Then they spread a blanket on the lawn and put the bouquet in the middle and they all sat down.

"Whatever are you wearing those shawls for?" asked Julia.

"And those rosettes?" asked Katie.

"K.O.S." answered Betsy and Tacy, rolling their eyes.

"K.O.S." answered Tib, trying not to laugh.

Julia and Katie went away.

"This is really a birthday party, isn't it?" asked Tib.

"Yes, it is," said Tacy. "And we ought to have a birthday cake."

"I can't very well ask my mamma for a birthday cake," said Betsy. "But I can ask for cookies and we can pretend they're cake."

That was what they did; and while they munched cookies they tried to imagine what was happening in Spain where the young Alphonso was ascending his throne.

"The newspapers tomorrow will have it all in," said Tacy from the depths of her shawl.

Tib put out a small perspiring face.

"But we ought to read them together," she said. "On account of our lodge. And we're never together on Sunday."

That was true. They attended different churches, and on Sunday afternoon they often went riding or visiting with their parents.

"Well, let's not look at the newspapers tomorrow," Betsy proposed. "And when our fathers have finished with them, let's save them."

"Then Monday, after school, let's take a picnic up on the Big Hill," suggested Tacy.

"Let's go to that place we went to before, where we can see Little Syria. It's the farthest from home of any place we know. There won't be anybody around to disturb us and Betsy can read the papers out loud," said Tib. "This mantilla's hot," she added.

"If you're going to be Queen of Spain," said Betsy, "you've got to get used to a mantilla. And so have Tacy and I, because we'll be your ladies-in-waiting, I suppose."

"Oh, of course," said Tib.

It was difficult next day not to look at the Sunday newspapers strewn so invitingly about. But they did not even peek; and when evening came they managed to hide away all the crumpled sheets.

Monday after school, carrying a picnic basket and a fat bundle of papers, they climbed the Big Hill.

They turned right at the Ekstroms' house, calling "hello" to their friend, Mrs. Ekstrom, who was weeding her garden. They went through the Secret Lane and past the Mystery House, down through a fold of the hills and up again. Then, leaving the thick-growing trees behind, they came out on a high rocky ridge just as they had done before.

Tib took the ends of her skirt into her hands. Holding them wide, as she did when she danced her Baby Dance, she ran to the edge of the ridge. Betsy and Tacy followed, and the three of them looked down over their discovered valley.

The hillside was freshly green now. The gardens of the Syrians made dark brown patches behind their little houses. Behind Mr. Meecham's Mansion an apple orchard made a patch of grayish pink. Everywhere wild plums, in dazzling white bloom, were perfuming the air.

"It's just a perfect place," said Betsy, "to read about his birthday."

Tacy and Tib thought so too.

They tucked the picnic basket into a cleft of the rocks behind them. Usually they ate their lunch as soon as they reached the place to which they were going, but today they were too anxious to read about the King of Spain.

Tib perched on a high boulder. Tacy sat down in the flower-sprinkled grass with her knees drawn into her arms. Betsy unfolded the newspapers and spread them on her lap. She leaned against a wall of rock and read:

" 'Eight grooms on horseback led the procession. The King rode in the royal coach with his mother, the Queen, and his youngest sister, the Infanta Maria Teresa. He was pale but perfectly cool.' "

"I wish we could have seen him," Tacy interrupted.

She gave a long, romantic sigh and looked at Tib. Taking the hint Tib sighed too.

" 'The King ascended the throne,' " read Betsy. " 'He bore himself with manliness. Smilingly he acknowledged the ovations of the crowd.' "

"What's 'ovations'?" asked Tib.

"It's cheering and clapping."

"We'd have clapped good and hard if we'd been there," Tacy said. "It's terrible that we weren't there."

Betsy read on: "'He wore a dark blue uniform with gold facings, a steel helmet with a white plume, and a red silk waist-band from which hung a sword.'"

"He must have looked stylish," Tacy said.

"Isn't there a picture?" Tib asked.

"Plenty of them. Here's a picture of the Palace. This is where you'll live, Tib," said Betsy.

"It looks like our post office, only bigger," Tib remarked.

"It's sure to be nice inside," said Tacy. "You'll like living there."

"'Speculation,'" continued Betsy, "'is rife in the capitals of Europe as to whom he will choose as a bride. . . .'" She paused and her gaze ran down the column.

"Don't read to yourself!"

"What is it?"

Betsy did not seem to hear. She gave a small squeak of dismay.

"Oh dear, dear, dear!"

"What *is* it?" cried Tacy and Tib.

"Tib can't marry him after all! None of us can!"

"Why not?"

"Because," wailed Betsy, "we're not of the blood royal."

"What does that mean?" Tib demanded.

"It means we're commoners."

"It means we're not princesses," Tacy explained. "He can only marry a princess."

"That's the silliest thing I ever heard of," said Tib. "Oh well! It doesn't matter. I'll wear my accordion-pleated dress when I dance my Baby Dance."

Betsy and Tacy looked at each other. Their eyes said, "Isn't that just like Tib?"

"But now we'll never see him!" cried Tacy in a tragic voice.

"Let's go over to Spain anyhow," said Betsy. "Let's be servants in the Palace if we can't be queen."

"You and Tacy wouldn't be any good as servants," said Tib. "You can't cook. I can cook, but I don't think it's worth while to go way over there just to cook."

They sat in a flat silence.

"It doesn't seem right," Tacy burst out, "that he doesn't know a thing about us. He ought to know there are such people as us, and that we have a lodge and wear his colors and pin his pictures to our under-waists."

"He certainly ought," Betsy agreed. An idea popped up in her head like a dandelion on a lawn.

"Let's write him a letter and tell him!"

"Betsy!" cried Tacy. "You wouldn't dare!"

"Do people write letters to kings?" asked Tib.

"If they want to they do. We do," Betsy said.

Tacy's blue eyes began to shine.

"We'd better do it right now," she said, "while Julia and Katie aren't around to catch on what we're doing."

"But we haven't any paper and pencil," said Tib.

"You can run to Mrs. Ekstrom's house and borrow some," said Betsy. "Tacy and I will wait right here."

Tib didn't mind going. She ran lots of errands for Betsy and Tacy. She was off now almost as swiftly as one of the little yellow birds which were flying in and out of the blooming wild plum trees.

When she was gone, Tacy said, "I certainly feel sorry about Tib's not being queen."

"So do I," said Betsy. "It's too bad we're not of the blood royal."

"She'd have made a nice queen," said Tacy, "in that accordion-pleated dress. And I've got kind of interested in queens. I wish we could think up another queen game so that Tib could be queen."

"Maybe we can," said Betsy. "There's a poem about Queen o' the May. Julia's reciting it for the School Entertainment. Maybe we can get an idea out of that."

They talked about it until Tib came back from Mrs. Ekstrom's.

She had a pencil and a tablet of paper, and an envelope too.

"I told Mrs. Ekstrom we were writing a letter. But I didn't say who to," she explained.

She sat down on one side of Betsy and Tacy sat down on the other. Betsy wrote the heading and the salutation just as she had been taught to do in school. Then she started the letter proper and when she couldn't think what to say next Tacy or Tib told her. When the letter was finished, it read like this:

Deep Valley, Minn.
May 19, 1902.

King Alphonso the Thirteenth,
Royal Palace,
Madrid,
Spain,
Europe.

Dear Sir,—

We are three little American girls. Our names are Betsy, Tacy, and Tib. We are all in love with you and would like to marry you but we can't, because we're not of the blood royal. Tib especially would like to marry you because she has a white accordion-pleated dress that she's going to wear when she dances the Baby Dance. She looks just like a princess. So we're sorry. But we're glad you got to be king. Three cheers for King Alphonso of Spain.

Yours truly,
Betsy Ray,
Tacy Kelly,
Tib Muller.

"That's a fine letter," said Tib.

"Tomorrow after school," planned Tacy, "we'll walk to the post office and mail it."

"We'll have to take some money out of our banks," said Betsy. "It will cost quite a lot of money, I imagine, to send a letter to Spain."

They put the letter into the envelope and sealed it and addressed it to the King in his Palace, Madrid, Spain, Europe.

45

When they had finished they were suddenly very hungry.

"I'm famished," said Betsy.

"I could eat nails," said Tacy.

"Let's have our picnic," said Tib. And they scrambled over the rocks to that cleft in a big rock where they had left their basket.

But when they reached the cleft they stared with eyes of wonder and dismay.

The picnic basket was gone!

IV

NAIFI

BETSY, Tacy, and Tib all had the same thought
. . . in the same instant too.

"Julia and Katie!"

"They were here! They were listening!"

"They heard us talking about the King of Spain."

It was a dark thought that sent a shadow over the golden afternoon. They looked at one another in horror, thinking how they would be teased. It would sound queer, said out loud in public, that they were in love with the King of Spain.

Tib bounded toward the path.

"Shall we chase them?"

"It wouldn't do any good," said Tacy.

"The sooner we don't see them the better, I think," said Betsy gloomily. "Gee whiz!" she added. Betsy very seldom said "Gee whiz!" She was too religious. But it was all she could think of to express her feelings now.

"Gee whiz!" repeated Tacy. "Gee whitakers!"

"Double darn!" said Betsy.

"We could get our lunch back anyway," said Tib. But neither Betsy nor Tacy paid any attention.

Tib bounced up and down.

"Let's look around," she said. "Maybe it wasn't them at all. Maybe it was a dog. . . ." She broke off in a squeal. "Look! Look! It is a dog, or something."

She dashed down the hill.

Betsy and Tacy ran around the rock. Halfway down the slope, worrying a basket, there was certainly a shaggy creature, the size of a large dog. But it wasn't a dog. It had horns.

"It's a wild animal, a jungle animal most likely,"

Betsy cried.

"Tib! Come back!" shouted Tacy.

But Tib continued to run headlong.

"It's a goat," she called back. "And he has our basket."

Betsy and Tacy weren't afraid of a goat. Besides, relief that Julia and Katie did not know their secret brought back their appetites. They ran after Tib who ran fiercely after the goat which bounded on small fleet hoofs over the tussocks of grass. The basket came unfastened, and a red and white fringed cloth flew out like a banner. Sandwiches, cookies, and hard-boiled eggs scattered in all directions.

"Oh! Oh! Oh!" panted Betsy and Tacy, pausing to pick them up. Tib did not pause. She chased the goat around some scrub oak trees, behind a clump of the white wild plum. Then. . . .

"Betsy! Tacy! Betsy! Tacy!" came Tib's voice, with something in it which caused Betsy and Tacy to drop the sandwiches again and run to find her.

They found her standing face to face with a little girl so strange that she seemed to have stepped out of one of Betsy's stories. Her dress had a long skirt, like a woman's, very full, made of faded flowered cloth. She wore earrings like a woman's too. A scarf was tied over her head. From a rosy-brown face very bright brown eyes darted from Tib to Betsy and Tacy.

Waving a stick in her hand, she began to talk excitedly. Not Betsy nor Tacy nor Tib could understand a word she said. She ran to the goat which had come to a standstill near by and shook her stick at it. She ran to the basket which he had dropped and then to some sandwiches which lay on the grass and began to pick them up swiftly. When she turned her back, Betsy, Tacy, and Tib could see that her hair hung in long black braids tied in red at the ends. Her shoes were red too, and under her dress she wore bloomers down to her ankles.

All this time she continued to pour forth a torrent

of loud, strange words. Betsy, Tacy, and Tib could not understand one of them but they knew what the little girl was trying to say. She was trying to tell them she was sorry that her goat had spilled their basket.

"It doesn't matter," said Betsy.

"We don't care a bit," said Tacy.

"We don't mind sandwiches being a little mussed. We often eat them that way," Tib explained.

The little girl kept right on saying loudly . . . they didn't know what.

She kept on picking up sandwiches and cookies and hard-boiled eggs, and finally Betsy and Tacy and Tib did the same. At last the lunch was restored to the basket, except one sandwich which the goat had gulped.

The goat now was as meek as Grandpa Williams' cow, nibbling the grass and paying no attention to them. The little girl pointed from the goat to the basket and shook her head until her braids swung out.

"She's the excitedest person I ever saw," said Betsy.

"She can't speak any English," Tacy said.

"Or understand it," said Tib.

All three stared at her, and unexpectedly she smiled. She showed white teeth, and dimples flashed in her round rosy-brown face.

"Isn't she darling?" cried Betsy. "Let's invite her to our picnic."

"How can we," asked Tib, "when she can't understand our language?"

"I know," said Tacy.

She shook out the red and white fringed cloth which she had just rescued and spread it on the grass. Betsy and Tacy took sandwiches and cookies and hard-boiled eggs and arranged them invitingly upon it. Then all three sat down, leaving one side of the cloth empty; and all three pointed from the little girl to the vacant place and back to the little girl again.

"Have a sandwich," said Tib, picking up the cleanest one she could find (it wasn't very clean) and offering it.

The little girl's smile gleamed whiter, her dimples flashed deeper than ever. She shook her head. Reaching into her girdle she brought out a chunk of cheese and a piece of a flat round loaf of bread. She sat down at the vacant place, her wide skirts billowing about her.

They had a picnic.

Betsy and Tacy had started picnicking when they were five years old, and Tib joined them soon after. They were all ten now, and they had had scores of picnics in the years between. But this was the most adventurous, the strangest, the funniest one they had ever had.

Trying to find a way to talk with their visitor, Betsy,

Tacy, and Tib pointed to the goat.

"Goat," they said. "Goat. Goat."

The little girl pointed to the goat. She said one word too, and they knew it meant "goat" in her language.

Betsy, Tacy, and Tib pointed to their sandwiches and to the thin loaf the little girl was eating.

"Bread," they said. "Bread. Bread."

The little girl pointed to their bread and hers. She said, they were sure, her word for bread.

A little yellow bird flew out of the white plum blossoms.

"Bird," said Betsy, Tacy, and Tib. "Bird. Bird."

The little girl said her word for bird. She laughed out loud, and they all laughed. They kept on saying words for a long time.

"Now we'll try something hard," said Betsy. And she jumped up. She pointed to herself. "Betsy," she said.

Tacy jumped up and pointed to herself.

"Tacy," she said.

Tib jumped up and pointed to herself.

"Tib," she said.

They did this two or three times.

Then the little girl got up. She bobbed a small bow. She pointed to herself, and her teeth and dimples flashed.

"Naifi," she said. Perhaps Betsy and Tacy and Tib were getting used to the sound of her strange language, but they understood the word. "Naifi," she repeated. They knew it was her name.

"Hello, Naifi," cried Betsy.

"Hello, Naifi," cried Tacy, clapping her hands.

"Hello, Naifi," cried Tib, jumping up and down.

"Hel-lo?" said the little girl, as though she were asking a question. She repeated the word several times. "Hel-lo? Hel-lo?"

Betsy pointed to herself.

"Say, 'Hello, Betsy.' "

"Say, hel-lo, Bett-see," Naifi said.

Betsy shook her head. She tried again.

"Hello, Betsy," she said, leaving out the "say."

This time Naifi got it right.

"Hel-lo, Bett-see," she repeated.

Tacy pointed to herself.

"Hello, Tacy."

"Hel-lo, Ta-cee," Naifi said.

"Hello, Tib," cried Tib.

"Hel-lo, Tib," said Naifi, looking very much pleased with herself.

Betsy and Tacy and Tib shouted, "That's fine!" And "Good for you, Naifi!"

"Hel-lo, hel-lo, hel-lo," said Naifi, as though she were practicing.

They had a lovely time, but at last Naifi sprang up, shaking out her skirts. She pointed to the goat and to the valley, with a stream of her strange, loud words.

"She means she must go home," said Betsy. "And we must too. Goodness! Look at the sun!"

While they were picnicking, the sun had gone half-way down the sky. That meant they must hurry for they were not allowed to stay up on the Big Hill after dark.

Naifi bobbed her little bob, showing her white teeth and dimples. She picked up her stick and waved it and called to her goat.

"Hel-lo," she called in farewell.

"You mean 'good-by,' " cried Betsy

"Good-by!" "Good-by!" cried Tacy and Tib.

They stuffed the red and white fringed cloth hurriedly into their basket and started up the hill, talking about Naifi.

"Is she a Syrian?" asked Tib.

"She must be," said Betsy. "She lives in Little Syria."

"She must have just come to America," said Tacy. "The other Syrians all know a little English and they don't dress like that."

"The women wear scarves on their heads when they come selling lace, though," Betsy said.

"Did you see her earrings?"

"And her red shoes?"

"They were beautiful."

"Why doesn't she come to our school, I wonder," Betsy asked.

"The Syrian children go to the Catholic School at the other end of town," Tacy replied.

They turned for a last look at the small gay figure, dimmed now by distance. A shadow lay on the valley. Mr. Meecham's Mansion led the row of little houses like a mother hen leading her chicks . . . safe home at dusk.

"We've got to *hurry*," said Tib. They started

climbing again. And presently something drove Naifi out of their minds.

Fluttering down the hill to meet them came a multitude of newspapers. They came like tumble-weed, blowing lightly about in all directions. With a shock Betsy and Tacy and Tib remembered the King of Spain.

Again they all had the same thought in the same instant.

"Our letter!"

"What became of it?"

"What did we do with it when we ran after the goat?"

Nobody remembered. Running up to the rocks, they began to search frantically but they could not find the envelope. Their high ridge had been swept bare by the wind.

"It was all addressed. Maybe someone will find it and mail it," Betsy suggested hopefully.

"It didn't have a stamp on it, though," said Tib. "And you said it cost a lot of money to send a letter to Spain."

"That's right," said Betsy. She stopped still. "Gee whiz!" she said.

"What's the matter?" asked Tacy.

"I hope the wind won't blow that letter where Julia and Katie can find it."

"We'd certainly never hear the last of it," said Tib.

Again dread like a cloud darkened the day.

It was darkening too from other causes. The sun, already low in the west, had dropped into a cloud-made pocket. The hilltop was windy and cold.

"I've got to get home," said Tib. "I get scolded if I'm not home on time."

"I get a pretty hard talking to," said Betsy.

"So do I," said Tacy.

They ran down the Secret Lane.

Halfway through it, they met Mrs. Ekstrom with an apron thrown over her head.

"I was looking for you," she said. "I was sure I hadn't seen you come past. Don't you know it's time you went home?"

"We're hurrying, Mrs. Ekstrom," Betsy said.

As they jogged down the Big Hill, they talked again about Naifi.

"Let's keep her a secret," Betsy said.

"Let's," said Tacy.

"And let's take the King of Spain's pictures out of our underwaists," said Tib, "as long as I can't be queen."

"You can't be *his* queen, but you're going to be a queen," said Betsy. "Tacy and I are planning it; aren't we, Tacy? Good-by," she panted, as their road met the path which led down to her home.

She raced past the barn and buggy shed where her father was unharnessing Old Mag. She darted among slim young fruit trees which looked chilly now in their pale pink and white finery, and skipped down the brown path dividing the kitchen garden. In the woodshed she paused to catch her breath.

She went into the kitchen softly, hoping that her late return would go unnoticed. As a matter of fact, it did. Her mother was busy, frying potatoes and listening to Julia rehearse the piece she was going to recite at the School Entertainment.

Julia loved to recite. Her loose dark hair scattered

on her shoulders, her face glowing, she went through her piece as though she were standing on a stage. She even made gestures.

Betsy sat down on the edge of a chair and listened. Secretly she admired Julia's reciting. It sent an icy trickle down her spine when Julia recited "Little Orphan Annie" and "The Raggedy Man." This new piece was different; it wasn't scary; but for Betsy it had a special value. Thinking of Tib she listened with pricked ears:

"You must wake and call me early, call me early, Mother dear,
　Tomorrow'll be the happiest time of all the glad New-year,
　Of all the glad New-year, Mother, the maddest merriest day,
　For I'm to be Queen o' the May, Mother, I'm to be Queen o' the May!"

V

THE SCHOOL ENTERTAINMENT

BEFORE the day of the School Entertainment it turned cold again. For a week rains drenched the hills, the terraced lawns, the sloping road of Hill Street. After the rains stopped, the skies were still overcast. It was pleasanter indoors than out and this was just as well, for everyone was busy getting ready for the School Entertainment.

Julia went about murmuring sweetly:

"For I'm to be Queen o' the May, Mother, I'm to be Queen o' the May."

Julia could hardly wait for the great day. Her feet loved a platform as Betsy's loved a grassy hill. Whether she was playing the piano, singing, or reciting, Julia was happy so long as she had an audience.

She was different in this from Katie who despised performing. For the Entertainment Katie was reciting Lincoln's Gettysburg Address. She knew every word of it; she could be depended upon not to make a single mistake. But she would not put in expression, no matter how much the teacher urged or coaxed.

Betsy and Tacy were singing a duet made up entirely of "meows." They were going to wear cat costumes cut from shiny black cambric, with cat ears and tails. Mrs. Ray and Mrs. Kelly were busy making the costumes and Mrs. Ray was busy too rehearsing Betsy and Tacy. They ran into difficulties for Betsy was singing alto. It was altogether too easy for her to slide up into the soprano part and sing along with Tacy.

When she did that, Tacy gave her a nudge which

meant, "Get back to your alto!" Betsy's mother sounded the right note hard and Betsy got back to her alto as quickly as she could.

At almost any time or place Tib might practice her Baby Dance. She would pick her skirt up by the edges and run and make a pirouette. This was the opening of her dance. There were five different steps and she did each one thirty-two times . . . a slide, a kick, a double slide, a jump step, and then a Russian step which was done in a squatting position kicking out first one foot and then the other. It was hard but Tib could do it.

Betsy and Tacy had seen her practice her dance on hill, lawn and sidewalk, but they had not yet seen the accordion-pleated dress.

"It's done," said Tib, the day before the Entertainment. "I'll be wearing it tomorrow when you call for me."

"We'll be there early," Betsy and Tacy said.

And next morning early they stopped at Tib's back door carrying their cat costumes in big cardboard boxes.

They wiped their feet hard on the mat and Matilda let them in. They ran into the back parlor and there stood Tib in her accordion-pleated dress. It was made of fine white organdie trimmed with rows of insertion and lace. A sash of pale blue satin was tied high in princess style. She wore a soft blue bow on her yellow curls.

Mrs. Muller, looking proud, turned her about for Betsy and Tacy to see.

"How do you like it?" she asked.

"It's beautiful," said Betsy.

Tacy only gazed, but with luminous eyes.

Tib lifted her skirt by the edges. She could hold it out wide because of the accordion pleats. She ran and made a pirouette.

"It's fine for my dance," she said, looking pleased.

"You can't put your grubby jacket on over that dress," Mrs. Muller said. "I'll let you wear my cape." And she left the room and came back with her best cape which was made of black lace trimmed with ribbons and rosebuds. "Take good care of it," she said, "and of the dress too. I'll see you at the Entertainment."

Betsy, Tacy, and Tib walked to school proudly. Betsy walked on one side of Tib and Tacy on the other.

The sun had come out in honor of the day. Snowball bushes nodded from the lawns, pansies and tulips in gardens looked festive with the sunshine on them, as though they knew about the Entertainment. The school steps were full of boys and girls looking unusually clean and dressed up. The upper grades were giving the Entertainment in the Seventh-Grade Room, which was the largest in the building. But all the rooms were open and ready for visiting mothers.

Betsy, Tacy, and Tib went first into their own Fourth Grade Room. It looked as dressed up as themselves. On Miss Dooley's desk was a bouquet of lady's slippers which one of the boys had brought. Samples of the children's work were pinned up on the walls. There were arithmetic papers and spelling papers, maps, charcoal drawings of cups and saucers, and paintings of oranges and apples.

Miss Dooley looked as dressed up as the room. Instead of her usual shirtwaist and skirt, she wore a flowing purple dress with large bell sleeves. Her hair was curled and her face was bright and anxious.

The class stayed in the Fourth Grade Room only long enough for prayer and roll call. Then Miss Dooley's bell tapped.

"Position! Rise! Turn! March!"

Someone was playing a march on the piano out in the hall. The Fourth Graders joined the other grades and they all marched into the Seventh-Grade Room.

It was crowded but that made the occasion all the gayer. Children sat double in the seats. Folding chairs had been brought in and mothers sat or stood around the walls. Betsy found her own mother sitting among the others. Betsy glanced at her, trying not to smile, and glanced away quickly, trying to act busy and important. Tacy and Tib were looking at their mothers and trying not to smile, too. All the mothers were dressed up and looked nice.

To open the Entertainment, all the children sang together. They sang "Men of Harlech" and it was fine. Then there was a play, and then Julia gave her recitation. Her recitation was different from other children's recitations; it always was. She did not seem like Julia at all as she stood up in front of the room. She looked frail and wistful, with her long hair full of flowers. She smiled and yet she seemed ready to cry. Her hands moved appealingly. Her voice was like spring rain:

> "Tomorrow'll be of all the year the maddest merriest day,
> For I'm to be Queen o' the May, Mother, I'm to be Queen o' the May."

"That child is certainly going to be an actress," Betsy heard one of the visiting mothers say to another visiting mother.

Betsy felt embarrassed and proud.

Soon after came Katie's turn. Square on her sturdy feet, her face scornful, she rattled without a mistake through the Gettysburg Address. She walked back to

her seat and sat down hard. When she had to take
bad medicine, Katie knew how to take it.

About that time Betsy and Tacy sneaked out to
the cloak room. Betsy's mother came too. While some
other children sang songs and spoke pieces and the
boy named Tom played a solo on his violin, Betsy and
Tacy put on their cat costumes. Mrs. Ray tied perky
red bows behind their tall cat ears.

Tom's solo ended and two large black cats jumped
out on the stage. Betsy's mother began to play the
piano and Betsy and Tacy began to sing:

"Mee-ee-ow! Mee-ee-ee-ow!"

Like a kettle boiling over, the room foamed with laughter.

And the louder the children laughed, the louder Betsy and Tacy made their caterwauls, the more they wiggled their ears and swished their tails. Sometimes Betsy slid up to the soprano and sang along with Tacy, but nobody cared. Tacy forgot to nudge her and Mrs. Ray forgot to pound the right note hard. When the Cat Duet ended, the children clapped and stamped. Mothers wiped tears of laughter from their eyes and Miss Dooley said:

"Betsy and Tacy will have to sing the Cat Duet again for us next year."

And so they did. In fact they sang it every year until they graduated from high school.

At the end of the program, Tib danced the Baby Dance. She ran out on the platform holding the accordion-pleated dress outstretched very wide. When she whirled, she looked like a butterfly. She did the first four steps, thirty-two times each, and when she began the Russian step, the hard one, squatting down and kicking out right and left, the audience began to clap. She went off the stage doing that step and the people clapped so hard that she had to come back to bow, holding the skirt out wide.

"She'll certainly make a good queen," Betsy whispered to Tacy as they clapped tired hands until they could clap no more.

The children marched back to their rooms after that. Mothers came visiting; it was like a big party. When the mothers left, the children returned to their desks briefly. Then Miss Dooley tapped her bell.

"Position! Rise! Turn! March!"

They marched out of the room and down the stairs.

On the front steps Betsy and Tacy took their places on either side of Tib. Still flushed from her dance, her eyes as blue as the soft blue bow which tied her curls, she looked pretty. But the accordion-pleated dress, alas, was covered up by the cape.

"Don't wear your cape home," said Betsy.

"I'll carry it for you," offered Tacy.

"Or I will," said Betsy.

Tib laughed.

"It seems funny to have you waiting on me," she said. "Usually I wait on you." It was true, and it was just like Tib to mention it.

Tib didn't feel any different or act any different because she looked so pretty and had danced so well.

"My mamma said I should take good care of this cape," she remarked, slipping it off.

"I'll take good care of it," promised Tacy. She folded it over her arm. Betsy took the cardboard boxes containing the cat costumes. They all walked proudly down the steps.

They skirted the sandy lot known as the boys' yard.
At the corner where it met the street a crowd of boys
had gathered. Although they were dressed in their
best clothes, they were acting very badly. They were
bouncing in a circle, yelling.

"They're teasing somebody," said Betsy.

"Mean things!" said Tacy.

"I wonder who," said Tib.

Coming nearer they could hear what the boys were
yelling. It was a singsong:

"Dago! Dago!"

"That's what they yell at the people from Little
Syria sometimes," said Tib.

"They yell it at Old Bushara and he chases them with a knife."

"Maybe it's Old Bushara in there now."

"Let's look! I've never seen him."

None of them had. They pushed into the crowd.

The victim they discovered was not Old Bushara. It was a little girl, a lone little girl, looking fearfully from face to face around the cruel circle. She wore a scarf tied closely around her rosy face, a wide long flowered skirt. . . .

"It's Naifi," cried Betsy and Tacy and Tib in one horrified breath.

Naifi saw them; she recognized them. Her eyes widened with hope.

"Hel-lo, hel-lo, hel-lo," she cried in agonized appeal.

Someone began to mimic her.

"Hel-lo, hel-lo."

"Oh dear!" cried Betsy, tears clouding her eyes.

The boy named Sam who had been chased by Old Bushara jumped out of the circle. He was in Fourth Grade along with Betsy, Tacy and Tib, but he was old enough to be in Seventh. He was big and rough. He snatched the scarf from Naifi's head and waved it. He pulled her long black braids.

Tacy struggled forward. She was shy but she wasn't shy enough to keep still now.

"You stop that!" she cried.

No one paid any attention to Tacy, except one boy who shouted, "Red-headed woodpecker!" because of her red curls.

Like a small shining comet Tib flashed into the ring.

"You let her go! You let her *be!*" she cried, pushing herself between Sam and Naifi. Sam pushed her back.

There was a singing sound. The accordion-pleated dress ripped smartly in his hand.

There was a scuffle then. Heedless of her dress, Tib

pushed Naifi through a break in the circle. Tacy ran to help; someone pulled her back; and Mrs. Muller's cape fell to the ground. Betsy couldn't let Tacy and Tib be so much braver than she was. She fought her way forward but she dropped the cardboard boxes. The two cat costumes, red ribbons and all, tumbled out.

With a shout Sam picked them up. Maybe he thought it would be fun to put on a cat costume. Maybe he was ashamed of himself and wanted an excuse to stop teasing Naifi. Certainly some of the other boys seemed ashamed.

Betsy, Tacy, and Tib surrounded Naifi and pushed her to the sidewalk.

"Run!" they whispered.

With one deep look of thankfulness, Naifi ran. A flash of blue bloomers, a gleam of red shoes, and she was gone.

Sam and another boy had put on the cat costumes.

"Mee-ow! Mee-ow!" they cried, prancing about.

A third boy was strutting up and down in Tib's mother's cape. Tib looked from that to her torn dress and her face went from red to white.

Betsy and Tacy started to cry, but they remembered they were ten years old and didn't. It was hard not to, though. And just at that moment who should come running but Julia and Katie. Big sisters arrive handily sometimes.

"You leave my little sister alone!" Betsy heard Julia shouting.

"Give me those costumes and that cape and be quick about it!" Katie said.

Everyone always minded Katie . . . even big boys . . . even Sam. Sam threw down the cat costumes and another boy tossed Tib's mother's cape into the air and ran. They all ran except a few of the boys who had looked ashamed. These helped to pick up the black costumes, the red ribbons, and the cape. Then they ran, too.

When they were alone, Betsy, Tacy, and Tib told Julia and Katie what had happened. But they did not tell them that they knew Naifi. Upset as they were, they remembered to guard their secret.

Katie shook out Tib's mother's cape.

"It looks as good as ever," she said.

"And we'll go home with you, Tib," said Julia, "to explain about your dress."

"I wish you would," said Tib.

She looked forlorn with her blue hair ribbon missing, her sash untied, and the torn skirt dragging on the ground.

Julia and Katie, Betsy, Tacy, and Tib walked slowly to the chocolate-colored house.

Julia explained the whole thing to Mrs. Muller.

She talked her prettiest, almost as though she were reciting; and she made Mrs. Muller understand.

"It's all right," said Mrs. Muller. "I'm glad Tib stood up for the little Syrian girl. Foreign people should not be treated like that. America is made up of foreign people. Both of Tib's grandmothers came from the other side. Perhaps when they got off the boat they looked a little strange too."

Tib looked at Betsy and Tacy. She breathed a long sigh of relief.

"But my dress, mamma!" she said. "Can it be mended?"

"Certainly it can be mended," Mrs. Muller answered.

"You'll have it to be queen in," Betsy and Tacy whispered.

For as soon as school was over, they intended to plan that game in which Tib would be queen.

VI

A QUARREL

THE queen game had an unexpected result.
It led to a quarrel with Julia and Katie.

Not an ordinary quarrel. Not one of the
kind which arose all the time from Julia and Katie
being bossy and Betsy and Tacy and Tib making

nuisances of themselves. Those quarrels didn't amount to much. They were always made up at bedtime with a pillow fight or a peace offering. Once when Julia had been mean, she bought Betsy a candy fried egg in a little tin pan . . . one cent at Mrs. Chubbock's store . . . to show she was sorry.

This quarrel was different. It lasted for days. Their fathers and mothers knew about it; the whole neighborhood knew about it. And while it was exciting at first, it made Julia and Katie and Betsy and Tacy and Tib all feel bad before it was ended. Julia and Katie were good big sisters, as big sisters go, and Betsy and Tacy were no more exasperating than other little sisters. Everyone liked Tib, and Tib despised quarrels. Yet Tib was the very center of this bitter feud.

The plan for a queen game lagged, after school ended. Betsy, Tacy, and Tib were busy enjoying not having to go to school. They climbed hills and trees, ate picnics, lay on green lawns and talked.

But they did not forget about queens. They could not. For Julia kept reminding them.

Julia kept on reciting:

"For I'm to be Queen o' the May, Mother, I'm to be Queen o' the May."

She recited it at the school picnic; she recited it

for the High Fly Whist Club to which her father and mother belonged; she recited it for the Masons and the Eastern Stars; she recited it for all the neighbors. Julia was a great reciter.

Betsy, Tacy, and Tib had queens on their minds, all right. But they did not do much about their plan for making Tib a queen, until they were jolted into it by Julia and Katie.

For several days Julia and Katie had been whispering together. And one hot noon at dinnertime, Julia asked permission to go down to Front Street with Katie. After dinner she shook all the pennies out of her pig bank, put on her hat, and borrowed her mother's parasol. She and Katie started down Hill Street looking superior.

"They've got something up their sleeves," Betsy and Tacy agreed as they sat with Tib beside Tacy's pump, washing carrots and eating them. The carrots were small and tender; they came from Tacy's garden. Washed in the cold well water, they made refreshing eating.

"Let's think up something ourselves," suggested Tacy. "What about that queen business . . . you know . . . making Tib queen of something?"

"That's just the thing," said Betsy.

"But what can I be queen of?" asked Tib. "I can't be queen of the May because it isn't May any more."

"Minnesota is too cold for May queens anyhow," said Tacy. "Look how cold it was last month."

"You can be a June queen," said Betsy. "I'll find out how they make May queens, and then we'll do just the same things only we'll do them in June. I'll go ask mamma about May queens now," she added, jumping up. She ran across the street to her home.

It was a good time to talk to her mother. Not only because Julia was out of the house, but because her mother was not busy. Mrs. Ray did her housework in the morning. After dinner she took a little rest, and after that she put on a fresh dress and sat down in the parlor. Sometimes ladies came to call.

No lady was calling today. Mrs. Ray rocked near a window from which she could look down Hill Street. She was keeping cool and embroidering the head of a Gibson Girl upon a pillow when Betsy burst into the room.

"Mamma," said Betsy. "Tell me about May Queens."

Mrs. Ray laughed.

"Queens! Queens! Queens!" she said.

Betsy thought that was a strange remark, but she persisted.

"How do people happen to have May queens?" she asked. "What do they do when they have them?"

"It's an English custom," answered Mrs. Ray,

working her needle skillfully in and out of the Gibson Girl's hair. "On May Day people used to go to the wood and bring back flowers. They called it 'going a Maying.' Then they put up a Maypole with garlands running from the top and danced around it. And they chose a pretty girl and crowned her with a wreath of flowers."

It sounded enchanting!

"I suppose," said Betsy eagerly, "people could 'go a Juning' and then crown a Queen of June."

"Of course they could," answered Mrs. Ray. "But

I *believe* that Julia and Katie have decided on a Queen of Summer."

Betsy jumped as though the needle in her mother's hand had pricked her.

"Haven't they?" asked Mrs. Ray looking up.

Betsy did not answer. She stared at her mother with horrified eyes.

Mrs. Ray put down her needle. She looked worried.

"You knew what they were planning, didn't you?" she asked. "If you didn't, I'm sorry. But you'd have known soon anyway. Julia is going to be queen. Katie and Dorothy and some of the rest of their friends are going to be maids of honor. And you and Tacy and Tib and Margaret are all going to be in it."

"We are, are we!" muttered Betsy.

"Tacy and I," she burst out, "are planning the same thing. We've been planning it for weeks and weeks. Only we're going to have Tib for our queen."

She jumped up, blazing. "Julia and Katie must have found out about it somehow. They're just copy-cats, that's what they are."

"I'm sure they're not," answered Mrs. Ray. "It all came from Julia's saying, 'I'm to be Queen o' the May' so much. She got the idea . . . or Katie did . . . that she ought to be queen of something."

She looked reprovingly at Betsy's dark face.

"I don't see why you feel so badly about it," she

said. "Julia and Katie are spending all their money to buy crepe paper and ribbons. You can all go in together and have a fine celebration."

Betsy did not answer. After looking blankly in her mother's face she rushed out of the room. She bounded over terrace, road and lawn.

"Tacy! Tib! Tacy! Tib!" she shouted wildly.

Tacy and Tib, who had been lying on their backs munching carrots, shot upright.

"I know something awful! Terrible!" Betsy cried. "Julia and Katie are planning a queen."

"A queen!"

"And Julia is going to be it!"

"The copycats!" cried Tacy. "However did they find out our idea?"

"I don't know. But they've gone downtown to buy crepe paper and ribbons. They're going to have a Maypole and Dorothy and the rest of the big girls are going to help them."

"We'll make ours just as nice," said Tacy stoutly. But in their hearts they doubted that they could. Big girls knew how to put on such shows better than younger girls did.

Their dismay was mixed with chagrin. They had had the idea of a queen for weeks and weeks. But they had not done anything about it. And while they were dawdling, Julia and Katie had made this lovely plan.

They had even taken money from their banks and gone downtown to buy crepe paper.

"They're planning to let us do some little thing," said Betsy bitterly, "along with Margaret and Paul and the rest of the babies."

"That's kind of them," said Tacy.

Tib looked from one to the other.

"Why not let Julia be queen if she wants to be?" she asked.

That was just like Tib! Betsy and Tacy would have none of such weakness.

"Has Julia got yellow hair?" demanded Betsy.

"Or an accordion-pleated dress?" Tacy wanted to know.

"Did she almost marry the King of Spain?" asked Betsy.

"No, sir," said Tacy. "You're the right one for queen."

Tib was silenced.

"We won't give in to those old copycats!" cried Betsy. And jumping up, she began to pump herself some water angrily. She made up a song as she pumped.

> "Copycats, copycats,
> Having a queen,
> Copycats, copycats,
> Just to be mean."

Tacy and Tib learned it and sang it with her. And the louder they sang, the angrier they grew. The warmer they grew too, and that helped to make them angrier. Even in the shade by the pump, bare legged and bare footed, they were very hot.

Julia and Katie looked extremely hot when they came toiling up Hill Street, laden with packages, under Betsy's mother's parasol. Betsy, Tacy, and Tib ran to meet them, singing at the tops of their voices:

> "Copycats, copycats,
> Having a queen,
> Copycats, copycats,
> Just to be mean."

"What under the sun are you yelling about?" asked Julia and Katie.

Betsy, Tacy, and Tib danced around them wrathfully.

"You know perfectly well what!"

"Tib's going to be queen!"

"Tib! Tib! Tib! And nobody can stop her!"

Julia and Katie looked at each other; they shook their heads sadly.

"Well, talk about copycats!" said Julia. "Getting up a queen just because we're getting up a queen."

"We thought of it first!" shrieked Betsy, Tacy, and Tib.

"We've been planning it," said Katie, speaking slowly and reasonably, "ever since Julia began reciting her piece."

"So have we! So have we!"

Julia and Katie looked at each other again. Their eyes seemed to ask, "Is that likely?"

This time Julia spoke, using that tone of gentle patience which Betsy, Tacy and Tib found particularly maddening.

"We were going to ask you in, you know. Just as soon as we got things planned. We were going to ask you to be flower girls."

Flower girls! That was the last straw.

In a rage Betsy snatched at the long roll of crepe paper under Julia's arm. She shouldn't have done it, but she did. Julia pushed her back, and Tacy snatched at Julia. Katie snatched at Tacy; and Tib, head first, butted in.

Margaret and Paul and the Rivers children came running. Mrs. Kelly and Mrs. Ray appeared on their porches. And just then Betsy's father came driving up the street. He said, "Whoa!" to Old Mag and stopped the buggy.

"See here! What's up?" he asked.

Betsy was crying and Julia was waving torn paper. Katie was boxing Tacy's ears, and Tib, very red in the face, was jumping up and down.

Mr. Ray wound the lines around the whip. He got out of the buggy and Old Mag found her own way up the little driveway that led to her barn.

Gripping Julia in one hand and Betsy in the other, Mr. Ray asked, "What's the matter?"

"Queen! Queen! Queen!" was all he could make out of their jumbled answers.

"Come along, all of you," he said; and, followed by the other children, he and Julia and Betsy went up to the front porch. He sat down there and loosened his collar. Mrs. Ray brought him some ice water.

"It's the most awful misunderstanding," she said.

"I'll clear it up," said Mr. Ray and he took a long drink of the ice water. "Now," he said. "What's it all about?"

Both sides told their stories.

Julia spoke last and she was near to weeping.

"Ordinarily," she said, "Katie and I would give in. We always do. But we've asked Dorothy and some other girls. What would they think? And we've spent all our money for crepe paper."

"Which maybe is spoiled," muttered Katie.

Betsy could see from her father's expression that this was a telling point.

"Well, Tacy and Tib and I can't give in," she

wailed. "We've been planning this since May seventeenth."

"May seventeenth?" asked Mr. Ray. "Why May seventeenth?"

"It just *was* May seventeenth," Betsy replied.

"Yes it was, Mr. Ray," Tacy and Tib added.

That was a good point too, remembering the day.

Mr. Ray thought for a long time. Mrs. Ray stood in the doorway looking worried, and there was a smell of biscuits baking. (For shortcake, probably.)

"It seems clear," said Mr. Ray at last, "that each side thinks his side is right."

Mrs. Ray nodded.

"And certainly," he continued, "there must be just one queen. Rival queens would never do."

He paused while the children stood in silence and Mrs. Ray waited in the doorway.

"I have it," he said. "We'll settle this in the good old American way."

"How?" all the children asked together.

"By the vote. By the ballot," answered Mr. Ray.

"But papa," said Julia. "That wouldn't do. Katie and I would vote for me, and Betsy and Tacy and Tib would vote for Tib."

"Let your friends vote," answered Mr. Ray. "Let the neighborhood vote."

He warmed to his idea.

"Take two sheets of foolscap," he went on, while

sniffs lessened and eyes brightened. "At the top of one write, 'We, the undersigned, want Tib Muller for queen.' And at the top of the other one write, 'We, the undersigned, want Julia Ray for queen.' Then tomorrow morning go out after votes. Take your papers up and down Hill Street. And may the best man win!"

It was a wonderful idea.

"Of course," said Mr. Ray, "you must be good sports. You must all agree to abide by the result of the vote. If Tib wins, Julia and Katie must pitch in and make a success of her coronation. And if Julia wins, Betsy and Tacy and Tib must be her loyal subjects. All right?" he asked.

"All right," everyone agreed.

"It's settled then," said Mr. Ray. He got to his feet. "Old Mag wants her supper and I do too."

"You're a perfect Solomon," said Mrs. Ray.

Katie and Tacy ran across the street and Tib skipped down Hill Street and home. Julia and Betsy and Margaret went into the house for supper, and there was strawberry shortcake.

At bedtime Mrs. Ray suggested to Betsy that she tell Julia she was sorry she had torn the crepe paper. Betsy told her, and Julia said it was perfectly all right.

Everyone thought that the quarrel was over. But it wasn't, somehow.

VII

OUT FOR VOTES

N THE Rays' hitching block next morning
Betsy, Tacy and Tib made out their petition. They printed at the top of a piece of
foolscap:

"We, the undersigned, want Tib Muller for
queen."

Across the street, on the Kellys' hitching block, Julia and Katie were printing on a sheet of foolscap too. Margaret and the Rivers children ran from group to group. Paul waited on the Kellys' porch with the dinner bell in his hand.

Katie called across the street, "Are families allowed to sign?"

"No! No!" whispered Tacy, nudging Betsy to remind her that Julia and Katie were on the Kelly side of the street; they could get to the Kelly house first and there were lots of people in the Kelly family.

"No," called Betsy. "Of course not." She and Tacy and Tib had finished. They jumped to their feet.

"No fair starting 'til the signal!" warned Julia. It had been agreed in advance that no one was to begin until Paul rang the dinner bell.

Betsy, Tacy, and Tib rocked impatiently on their toes; Julia and Katie jumped up.

"Ready?" cried Paul. "One, two, three, go!"

He rang the bell vigorously, and the race for votes was on.

With excited whoops both sides started running down the sloping sun-dappled street. Julia and Katie ran on the Kellys' side; Betsy, Tacy, and Tib, on the Rays' side.

Betsy, Tacy, and Tib paused to sign up the oldest Rivers child. She hadn't started to school yet but she could print her name. They ran into the Riverses' house and Mrs. Rivers signed. They ran down the terrace to the next house.

In that house lived a deaf and dumb family. That is, the father and mother were deaf and dumb. The baby cried as loudly as any other baby. Their name was Hunt. Mrs. Hunt had taught Betsy and Tacy the alphabet in sign language. So they asked her in sign language to vote for Tib for queen. They showed her the petition too, and pointed to Tib and said, "Vote!" Mrs. Hunt smiled and wrote her name.

Betsy, Tacy, and Tib bounded down the terrace to the Williamses' blue frame house. They called there sometimes to borrow the Horatio Alger books. These belonged to Ben who walked home from school with Julia. His sister, Miss Williams, was Julia's music teacher.

Ben said that he was too busy to vote. He looked cross. Miss Williams wouldn't sign either. She exclaimed, "Why, Julia has been planning for weeks on being the queen!" Mrs. Williams signed though, and Grandpa Williams signed. So they came out even.

Across the street Julia and Katie could be seen at Mrs. Benson's door.

"She won't sign, I'll bet. She'll wait for us," said Tacy as she and Betsy and Tib leaped down another terrace to the Grangers' house.

This was a neat light tan house with brown trimmings. No children lived there; the Granger daughters were grown up. But Betsy and Tacy knew the house well, for here they often borrowed *Little Women*. They had borrowed it almost to tatters.

Mrs. Granger signed and so did the woman in the house below. She had two small children . . . not old enough to print their names.

In the last house of the block lived a family with many children. All of them signed.

Betsy, Tacy, and Tib paused, panting and triumphant. Julia and Katie emerged from the last house in the block on their side and ran into the vacant lot which led to Pleasant Street.

Here both parties sighted the familiar stocky figure of Mr. Goode, the postman.

Mr. Goode had been bringing the mail to Hill Street for years. He was the children's friend. Julia and Katie, Betsy, Tacy, and Tib ran toward him as though running for a prize. They all fell upon him at once.

Mr. Goode read both petitions.

"I'll sign both or none," he said. So they let him sign both. But when he had passed on up Hill Street they decided not to let anyone else sign both petitions.

"It would mix things up," Katie explained. "We

wouldn't know at the end who had won."

Betsy and Tacy and Tib agreed.

"Ta, ta," said Julia and Katie, and they cut through the vacant lot to Pleasant Street. One of their best friends lived on Pleasant Street. She was the Dorothy whom they had included in their plans for a queen celebration. Her father and mother played with Betsy's father and mother in the High Fly Whist Club.

Julia and Katie were certainly heading for her house.

"Let's fool them," said Betsy. "Let's us go to Pleasant Street too. We'll go the other way."

So they raced back up Hill Street and went to Pleasant Street by the road which led down the Big Hill past Tacy's house. At that corner lived the little girl named Alice. She was an earnest little girl with fat yellow braids.

"I'll come along and help," she said.

"Come along," said Betsy, Tacy, and Tib.

They started down Pleasant Street with Alice.

And, just as they had expected, they found Julia and Katie at Dorothy's door.

"Ya, ya! Fooled you!" yelled Betsy, Tacy, and Tib.

"Copycats!" yelled Julia and Katie.

"Copycats!" echoed Dorothy. She was one of the little girls' favorite big girls, with brown curls and eyes and a very sweet voice. But she was their enemy now.

They were all having fun, though.

"How many votes have you got?" yelled Betsy.

"Show us your list and we'll show you ours," yelled Julia and Katie.

They met in the middle of the road and compared lists. Julia had fifteen votes for queen, but Tib had sixteen.

"It's certainly close," said Alice.

The two parties separated and ran from door to door.

They both rushed at the baker's boy when they saw him coming out of a house with his tray full of jelly rolls and doughnuts. He was a fat boy with red cheeks; they knew him well.

Like the postman he wanted to sign both lists. But they wouldn't allow it.

He looked from Julia with her loose brown hair on her shoulders to Tib with her crown of yellow curls.

"By golly!" he said. "This is fierce!"

After a moment he signed Julia's list.

"But I'll give you a doughnut," he said to Tib.

She divided it with Betsy, Tacy, and Alice.

The two parties made rushes also at the grocer's boy, the butcher's boy, the iceman, and the milkman. Up and down Pleasant Street they went. They were amazed when the whistles blew loudly for noon. They ran home in great good humor and Julia and Betsy told their adventures at the dinner table.

Mr. Ray winked at Mrs. Ray.

"See!" his wink seemed to say, "I straightened everything out!"

"You must be almost ready to stop and count votes," he said.

"Oh no, papa!" cried Betsy.

"But you must have called on everyone you know?"

"Why, papa!" said Julia. "We haven't been to

School Street yet. Some of my best friends live on School Street."

"Well, I don't want you to go too far away," said Mrs. Ray. "How far do you think they should be allowed to go, Bob?"

"Not beyond Lincoln Park," said Mr. Ray.

Lincoln Park was a pie-shaped wedge of lawn with a giant elm tree and a fountain on it. Hill Street turned into Broad Street there. It was the end of the neighborhood.

"Lincoln Park, then," said Mrs. Ray. "But before you start out, I want you to wash and wipe the dishes. I have to frost the cake I'm sending to the Ice Cream Social."

Julia's eyes widened.

"Where is the Social, mamma?"

"It's on the Humphreys' lawn," said Mrs. Ray. "They're raising money for the Ladies Aid."

She had made a layer cake with lemon filling, and she frosted it with thick white frosting while Julia and Betsy washed the dishes. By the time they were finished, Katie and Tacy and Tib were yoo-hooing from the hitching block.

The two parties started out again.

Unlike Julia and Katie, Betsy, Tacy, and Tib had no friends on School Street, but they went there just the same. They wanted to keep Julia and Katie in sight. They could see them, on the opposite side of the street, running busily from house to house.

Betsy, Tacy, and Tib went from house to house too. And this was a different business from calling at the houses on Hill Street. It was fascinating, delicious, to knock at the doors of houses whose outsides they had known for years but whose insides were unknown and mysterious.

There was the red brick house with limestone trimmings where they had always imagined very wealthy people lived; there was the house with pebbles set in plaster above the door; the house with an iron deer on the lawn; the house where bleeding hearts grew in the spring.

Some of these houses they had always loved; some they had almost feared. They had never expected such luck as to see inside them all. Opening doors gave glimpses of strange faces, of banisters leading mysteriously upstairs, of an organ, of a hired girl in a cap.

A few ladies slammed doors or said they were busy, but most of them signed the paper, voting for Tib. One told the children to wait and brought cookies. Another, a plump young woman, said she had just made fudge; she gave them some.

"I like going out for votes," said Tib, happily eating her fudge.

They were enjoying themselves so much that they did not notice when Julia and Katie dropped out of sight. But all at once they realized that their rivals were nowhere to be seen.

"They've cut through lots somewhere," said Betsy.

"They've lost us on purpose, I'll bet," Tacy said. "Where do you suppose they've gone?"

"I don't know," said Betsy. "But I think we'd better go around this corner and keep on as far as Lincoln Park."

That was what they did. But now the ladies in the houses at which they called said that Julia and Katie had been there.

"May we sign your list too?" they asked.

"No, ma'am. We have an agreement."

They were growing warm. They were a little tired too, and more than a little dirty.

Lincoln Park came into sight, cool and green under its elm, the waters of its fountain sparkling.

"Let's stop and rest before we go home," said Betsy.

"Look there!" Tib cried. "What's going on at the Humphreys' house?"

"It must be a wedding or a funeral," said Tacy.

Betsy remembered.

"It's the Ice Cream Social. They're raising money for the Ladies Aid. Mamma baked a cake for them."

They stared at the Humphreys' house, a large yellow stone house that overlooked the Park. The road before it was crowded with carriages and the lawn was crowded with tables. Ladies in light summer dresses trailed over the grass.

"It looks pretty," said Betsy.

"I wish we had money to buy some ice cream," said Tacy.

It was Tib this time who had an idea.

"We could get votes there," she said. "Lots and lots of votes. Enough to win."

Betsy and Tacy paid her idea the tribute of enraptured silence.

"Just pass the paper around," Tib explained, thinking that they did not understand.

"Tib!" cried Betsy then. "That's a wonderful plan!"

"Julia and Katie will be frantic," Tacy cried.

"You're the one to do it, Tib," said Betsy. "You're so little and cute."

"I'm dirty though," said Tib. And she certainly was. There was chocolate on her face, chocolate on her hands, and chocolate on the front of her dress.

"We'll go over to the Park," said Betsy, "and you can wash up in the fountain."

They ran across the street to Lincoln Park, and Tib washed her face and hands in the fountain. Betsy and

Tacy picked a bouquet of clovers and pinned it over the chocolate spot on the front of her dress.

"Now," they said. "You look fine."

Tib took the paper and pencil and ran lightly across to the Social.

She was pleased to be going. People made a fuss over Tib because she was little and cute. She wasn't conceited about it but she liked it. She was certain now, and so were Betsy and Tacy, that she would come back with the signature of every single person at the Social.

Betsy and Tacy lay down beneath the elm. They stretched their tired bodies on the turf and gazed into the remote green branches. They did not speak, but they shared a great content.

This was shattered almost immediately and most unexpectedly by Tib's return. She arrived at a run, very red of face.

"You come with me!" she said. "Just come with me!"

Betsy and Tacy jumped to their feet and followed her back across the street.

"Look there!" said Tib, pointing to the Humphreys' lawn.

They followed her indignant finger.

A near-by table was covered with a snowy cloth. There was a big bouquet of roses in the center. Sit-

ting at the table looking very grown up, eating ice cream and helping themselves freely to cake, were Julia and Katie.

Their paper and pencil lay on the table between them.

Catching sight of Betsy, Tacy, and Tib, Julia lifted the paper and waved it.

"Don't bother to come in," she said. "We've got all the names."

"And Mrs. Humphreys just insisted," said Katie, "that we have some ice cream."

"Oh! Oh! Oh!" cried Betsy, Tacy, and Tib. They rushed furiously away.

They did not return to the Park. That cool green-ness did not suit their rising temper. They began the long hot plod up Hill Street, raging.

"That's why they ducked us."

"I knew they were trying to."

"Julia asked Mamma this noon where the Social was going to be held."

"She was planning it then."

"It's the meanest thing I ever heard of."

"Of course," said Tib, "we were going to do the same thing ourselves."

Betsy and Tacy closed their ears to that remark. (It was just like Tib to make it.)

"They must have gotten a hundred names," said Betsy.

"We can never, never, never catch up."

"Gee whiz! Gee whitakers! We've got to."

"But there aren't any more names to get. We can't go beyond Lincoln Park," Tib reminded.

This time Betsy had the idea. She stopped still, planting her feet hard.

"We can't go beyond Lincoln Park," she said. "All right! We'll turn around and go back. And we'll just keep on going."

"But Betsy," said Tib. "There's no sense in that. We'll come to the hills."

"And we'll just keep on going," Betsy repeated.

Tacy did not speak at once. Her eyes began to sparkle.

Tib tried to puzzle it out.

"Of course there's the Ekstroms' house, up on the Big Hill. But there wouldn't be many votes there."

"You mean we should go to Little Syria!" said Tacy.

"Little Syria?" cried Tib.

Betsy nodded, her face tight with glee.

"I've always wanted to go there," Tib cried joyfully. "I'm not afraid of Old Bushara."

"We'll see Naifi too."

"And think of the votes! I'll bet there are more votes in Little Syria than there are at any old Ice Cream Social."

"It will serve Julia and Katie just right."

"We'll have to keep it a secret from them that we're going though."

"We'd better keep it a secret from everybody," said Betsy. "Of course we've never been forbidden to go. But then, nobody ever thought we *would* go."

"We'd better just go," said Tib. "Tomorrow morning! Take a picnic!"

They walked briskly, smiling, up Hill Street.

That night at supper Mr. Ray asked who was ahead

in the queen-race.

"Julia, I think," said Betsy, as though it didn't matter much.

"Are you ready to count votes and decide?" asked Mr. Ray.

"Not quite," said Betsy. "But Julia's certainly ahead. She's got a big long list."

Mr. Ray looked at Mrs. Ray proudly. His lips formed the words, "Good sport!"

Julia looked at Betsy sharply. Betsy's face was innocently bright.

VIII

LITTLE SYRIA

WHEN Betsy, Tacy, and Tib started out next morning, Julia and Katie were sitting on the Rays' side lawn making streamers. It was a shining morning. The rose bush under the dining-room window was covered with yellow roses which gave out a spicy smell. Julia and Katie were having a good time, twisting pink and green paper and making plans for Julia's coronation. They were very good natured for they were sure that Julia had won.

"Going for a picnic?" Julia called kindly as Betsy, Tacy, and Tib went past with their basket.

"Might as well," Betsy answered, trying to sound glum.

"You can get the Ekstroms' votes while you're up on the Big Hill," reminded Katie.

"That's so," Tacy replied.

"Try to make your backs look discouraged!" Betsy whispered. And she and Tacy and Tib all let their shoulders sag. Tib gave a loud sniff as though she were crying. Tacy put her arm around Tib's shoulder.

Julia and Katie looked after the three forlorn figures, and suspicion arose in their faces.

"They're up to something," Katie said firmly.

"Never mind," said Julia. "They couldn't get enough votes. Nobody lives up on the Big Hill except the Ekstroms."

"That's right," Katie said.

She and Julia went back to twisting streamers.

Betsy, Tacy, and Tib trudged on up the hill.

Their backs drooped in sadness, but their faces were wide with smiles.

"They'll be plenty surprised when we come home,"
said Tacy as they climbed past the ridge where wild
roses were in bloom. The air was freshly sweet with
the smell of these blossoms. Flat, pink and golden-
centered they clambered everywhere.

The grass was full of country cousins of the flowers
down in Hill Street gardens. There were wild gera-
niums and wild sweet peas and wild morning glories.
Betsy, Tacy, and Tib picked bouquets and gave them
to Mrs. Ekstrom when they offered her their petition.

Mrs. Ekstrom put on her spectacles to read it.

"Queens, eh?" she said. "How do you get so interested in kings and queens? I thought we left kings and
queens behind in the old country."

But in spite of her teasing, she signed her name.
She signed it with pen and ink.

Betsy, Tacy, and Tib went on, through the shadowy
Secret Lane, past the Mystery House, down through
a fold in the hills and up again. They came out as
usual on the high rocky point which overlooked the
now familiar valley.

They felt as though it belonged to them, this wide
green hammock stretching from sky to sky. They
gazed on it with pride for never had it looked so lovely
as it looked now clothed in summer green. Thickly
leaved trees almost concealed Mr. Meecham's Mansion and the row of little houses. But the roof tops

were visible.

Tib counted them.

"There are thirteen," she said. "Is our paper long enough, Betsy, for all the names we'll get?"

"I brought an extra sheet," said Betsy. "Just to be sure."

They ate their picnic quickly, tucked their petition and pencil into the empty basket, and started down the slope.

They descended boldly, yet with fast-beating hearts. Well they knew they were not supposed to be going to Little Syria, alone, on foot! They passed the clump of wild plum trees where they had picnicked with Naifi and looked about for the goat, but it was nowhere to be seen.

"I'm glad Naifi lives there," said Tacy. It was good to think of a friend awaiting them in the strange place to which they were going.

"I wonder whether she's learned to speak English yet," said Tib.

"Probably a little by this time," said Betsy. "Papa says it's wonderful how the Syrians get ahead."

Their feet were now on the path leading down to the settlement. It was just a row of small houses facing that eastern hill which Betsy, Tacy, and Tib were cautiously descending. They were ramshackle houses, much in need of paint. Here were no well-tended lawns or flower gardens as on Hill Street. Just sun-baked dirt yards, and morning glories twining over a few of the porches.

There were vegetable gardens, however. People were working in them, and their voices rose, loud and harsh, speaking in a foreign tongue.

"I wonder which house Old Bushara lives in," said Tacy nervously.

"Let's go first to Mr. Meecham's. He can speak English," Betsy said.

They left the path and walked along the hillside parallel to the street. Mr. Meecham's Mansion faced west, so they came upon it from the rear.

It did not look hospitable. The buildings and grounds were enclosed in a high iron fence with spikes along the top. Moreover it was studded with signs which said bluntly, "No trespassing!" "Keep out!"

The fence was freshly painted and in excellent re-pair. Inside it, however, everything looked shabby and untidy. The big white barn with lightning rod atop, the carriage house, and woodshed needed paint as badly as the Syrian houses did. A broken wagon and some rusted tools lay in the barnyard.

"Mr. Meecham doesn't seem to take much interest in anything but his fence," said Tib, peeking through the narrow iron bars.

"I wish we could see his white horses," said Tacy.

"I don't believe they're there," said Betsy. "The carriage-house door is open and there's no carriage inside."

"Let's go around to the front gate," said Tib.

They followed the high iron fence around to the street.

The empty sunlit valley stretched away to the south. And the dusty street of little houses stretched away to the north. No one was in sight except some children playing and a young man who was chopping wood near the small house opposite.

Betsy, Tacy, and Tib stared at Mr. Meecham's gate. It was closed and looked forbidding. Within, through a weedy overgrown lawn, an avenue of evergreen trees led the way to the house.

"Those evergreens," said Tacy, "remind me of a cemetery."

"Maybe we shouldn't bother with Mr. Meecham's vote," suggested Betsy.

"Why not?" asked Tib.

"Well, there are some more of those 'No Trespassing' signs."

"We're not trespassers. We're callers," said Tib. And swinging her body lightly, as she did when she was gathering courage, she lifted the latch. It opened, and she stepped inside. Betsy and Tacy followed. But none of them liked it when the gate with a loud clang shut behind them.

The avenue of evergreen trees was like a tunnel. As Betsy, Tacy, and Tib walked slowly into its aromatic darkness they seemed to leave behind all the brightness of the sweet June day.

"I wonder," said Tacy, "whether Mr. Meecham really cares who's queen."

"Probably," said Betsy. "He doesn't care a bit."

"Well, we care," said Tib.

They kept on going forward.

The gray brick house had tall arched windows which looked like suspicious eyes. It was shabby and unkempt. Ragged clumps of honeysuckle fell over the doorway but its penetrating sweetness seemed to be wasted. The windows were all closed and the shades pulled down.

Betsy and Tacy looked at each other, but before either one could think of an excuse for turning back, Tib had tripped up to the door. She pulled the rusty iron bell. A peal resounded hollowly within.

"Nobody's home. We might as well go away," said Betsy after a quarter of a second.

"Maybe somebody's home," said Tib, and pulled the bell again.

"Don't bother to ring," said Tacy hastily. "I'm sure nobody's home."

But somebody was at home.

At that moment a large, dirty, ugly-looking dog swept around the house. Barking furiously, he took his stand in the driveway.

Even Tib looked dismayed for a moment. Tacy stepped forward, for she liked dogs and they usually liked her.

"Here, doggie! Good doggie! Nice doggie!" said Tacy. But the dog did not seem to like being called doggie. He stood on stiff angry legs, his head out-thrust, looking as big as a horse. He showed his fangs and barked louder than ever.

"We'd better run," said Tib.

They took to their heels and the dog ran in pursuit. Never had sunlight looked so welcome as that bright arch which showed the end of the avenue of evergreens.

Rushing ahead of Tib the dog reached the gate first. He barked so angrily that Tib did not dare to touch the latch.

"Climb!" she cried, heading for the fence at the left of the gate. She was carrying the basket and she threw it over. Then she caught at the crosswise bar and pulled herself up.

Betsy and Tacy tried to do the same. They did it! They got to the top with the dog at their heels and slid down the outer side. But Betsy's dress and petticoats caught on the spikes. She hung like a scarecrow.

Tacy and Tib would have rescued her in time but they did not have to try. The man who had been chopping wood ran across the street. He lifted her down in a twinkling and set her on the ground. Tacy and Tib helped to smooth down her skirts. They were not too badly torn.

"Th-th-thank you!" said Betsy.

"You're welcome. Don't mention it," the young man answered. His speech had a foreign twist but they could understand him. He had thick black hair like a cap, and a dark merry face.

"What are you three little girls doing here?" he asked.

"We're out for votes," said Tib.

"Votes? For what?"

"For queen," said Tib. She found the basket, pulled out the list and handed it to him.

The young man looked perplexed. He glanced at the paper.

"Tib?" he said. "Which one is Tib?"

"I am," said Tib, looking at him with a smile.

"And is one of you Bett-see? And one Ta-cee?" he asked.

"Yes. How did you know?"

Striding across the narrow street, he called loudly, "Naifi!" He turned back, smiling. "I am Naifi's father," he said. "And I am very glad to meet the three little girls who were so kind to her."

Betsy, Tacy, and Tib were gladder than he was.

A little girl ran out of the house. At first they did not think it was Naifi, for she wore quite an ordinary short dress like their own and ordinary shoes and stockings. But she had Naifi's earrings, and her long dancing braids, and her dancing eyes, and her dimples.

Naifi stood smiling at them, and they at her. Her father had never stopped smiling. The place where they stood in the road was warm with smiles.

Naifi's father spoke first in Syrian, then in English. "These are your friends, my heart, my eyes?" he ended.

Naifi answered in Syrian.

"Speak English," he said. "You know you can speak it a little. And you are learning fast.

"She is now a little American girl," he said to Betsy, Tacy, and Tib. "She does not wear any more the old country clothes to be teased by bad boys. If she had a mother, she might have changed them quicker. But I am only a father. I am stupid. When her mother died, I came here from Syria and left Naifi behind. I and my father came, and Naifi stayed with my mother. But this year when we earned money enough, we sent for them."

Pushing Naifi gently he said, "Take your friends

inside to your grandmother, my little love, my eyes."

Betsy whispered to Tacy, " 'My eyes!' Isn't that a funny pet name?"

"Well," said Tacy thoughtfully, "there is nothing more important than your eyes. And I guess that's what he means when he gives that pet name to Naifi."

They followed Naifi across the narrow porch and entered the parlor of her house. It had chairs, a table, a carpet, and a lamp hanging by chains from the ceiling. It was almost like any other parlor. And yet not quite.

A low bench with pillows on it ran around the

walls. And a bony old man, wearing a round red cap with a tassel, sat on the floor, cross-legged, smoking a pipe. It was a curious looking pipe. It stood on the floor, more than a foot high; a long tube led away from it, ending in the old man's mouth.

"That is a narghile," said Naifi's father, noticing their interest. "He draws the smoke through water, and it makes the sound you hear. You Americans call it a hubble-bubble pipe."

It was, in fact, making a sound like hubble bubble.

"He is Naifi's grandfather," Naifi's father said.

The old man took his pipe out of his mouth and said, "How you do?" and smiled. He had strong white teeth, as though he were not old at all.

Naifi led them on to the kitchen which was just behind the parlor. And here an old lady was sitting on the floor! She was sitting in front of a hollowed-out block of marble in which she was pounding something with a mallet.

"She is making kibbee," explained Naifi's father. "That is meat she is pounding; it is good lean lamb. She is Naifi's grandmother," he said.

He spoke to the grandmother in Syrian, and she got to her feet. She was a tiny old lady with a brown withered face like a nut. She wore earrings, and the same sort of long full-skirted dress that Naifi had worn the first time they saw her. She could not say even "How you do?" in English, but she made them welcome with excited gestures.

Betsy, Tacy, and Tib looked with all their eyes.

Naifi led them out of the kitchen into the sunny back yard. The goat was tethered there.

"Goat!" said Naifi. "Goat! Goat!"

She laughed, and they all laughed, remembering the English lesson. The goat looked at them with wise, mischievous eyes. He seemed to remember he had stolen their basket.

The grandmother came hurrying out with a glass jar in her hand. She opened it and passed it about. Betsy, Tacy, and Tib helped themselves to raisins.

"Raisin," said Naifi, holding one aloft.

Then the grandfather appeared. Standing, he was even more amazing than sitting, for he was very tall. He wore full trousers, gathered at the ankles, and he had not doffed his red be-tasseled cap. He shouted loudly, and the grandmother ran into the house. She came back with a second glass jar which she opened and passed. This one was full of dried figs.

"Figs," said Naifi proudly, smiling.

The grandfather looked pleased, and so did the grandmother. So did Naifi's father who joined them, and so did Naifi. When they had finished eating raisins and figs Naifi's father said, "Now tell me about this paper you have brought. What is it you want?"

Betsy explained about the election, and he listened seriously.

"I do not think," he said, "that queens are good to have. But Tib is my Naifi's friend. If she wants my vote, here it is."

Taking the pencil he wrote his name carefully. He wrote from right to left.

He explained the matter in Syrian to the grandfather, the grandmother and Naifi. And the grandfather signed the list; the grandmother signed the list; and Naifi signed the list. They all wrote from right to left.

Afterward Naifi's father talked a long time in Syrian. He talked in a loud harsh voice, but not an angry one, waving his arms. The grandfather, the grandmother and Naifi all talked too. All of them waved their arms and acted excited.

There was a pause; then Naifi's father smiled at Betsy, Tacy, and Tib and said in English, "Naifi will take you to all our friends and neighbors. All of them will sign . . . those who can write. You three little girls were kind to my little girl, and the Syrians will sign your paper."

It was an adventure, getting the votes. With Naifi guiding them, Betsy, Tacy, and Tib went to every one of the little Syrian houses. They went into parlors, kitchens, gardens. They saw people drinking coffee, poured from long-handled copper pots into tiny cups. They saw women baking flat round loaves of bread such as Naifi had eaten the day they picnicked together, and other women making embroidery, and men playing cards. They saw a boy playing a long reed flute . . . a munjaira, Naifi said it was. They saw everything there was to be seen and they met everyone and everyone signed. Most of them wrote from right to left.

"I wonder why they write from right to left," said Tib.

"That is Arabic writing," one of the Syrians explained. "The Syrian language is Arabic."

Most of them spoke and understood English, but some of them did not. There was much loud harsh talk, but now Betsy and Tacy and Tib understood that that was just the sound of the Syrian language. There was much excited gesturing, stamping, and running about, but now they understood that that was only the Syrian way.

The houses were crowded, for sometimes more than one family lived in a house. There were many children in every family too. The paper was soon filled with names. They had to use the extra paper. Betsy was glad she had brought it.

At last all the people in the settlement had signed. It was time to go home.

Betsy and Tacy and Tib were ready to start. They had said good-by to Naifi's tall grandfather and her tiny wrinkled grandmother, to her merry father with his black hair like a cap, to Naifi and the goat. They had said "thank you" for the raisins and figs and were just stepping off the porch when they heard cries up the street.

Looking in that direction they saw Syrian children scrambling out of the road. They saw a cloud of dust and heard the thud of hoofs. A team of glossy white horses flashed into view. They were driven by a coach- man who wore a plug hat like a coachman in a parade. A glittering open carriage swayed along the narrow street. Betsy, Tacy, and Tib glimpsed a white beard . . . a black veil. Here were Mr. Meecham and his daughter!

The carriage stopped at Mr. Meecham's gate, and the coachman sprang down. He unlatched the gate and was about to ascend to his seat when Tib darted forward.

"Please, Mr. Meecham," she said, "will you sign my petition so I can be queen?"

"Eh? What?" asked Mr. Meecham. He sounded as though he could not believe his ears.

His bearded face was stern and scornful. His daughter did not lift her veil, but she leaned forward curiously.

Tib stood in the road beside the carriage, the sun on her yellow curls.

"I want to be queen," she said, handing him the paper.

Mr. Meecham read the petition. He looked at Tib, and at Betsy and Tacy; and above the snowy Niagara of his beard a smile began to form.

Mr. Meecham took out a gold pencil.

"I'll sign with the greatest of pleasure," he said.

And he signed. And so did his daughter. And so did his coachman.

Betsy, Tacy, and Tib climbed the hill in a glow of satisfaction.

"Wasn't it lovely!" Betsy sighed.

"Wasn't it nice!" said Tacy.

"I like Little Syria," said Tib. "I always said I . . ."

She stopped without finishing her sentence. She whirled around and looked toward the valley.

"Where," she demanded. "was Old Bushara?"

Where, indeed!

They looked down on the thirteen rooftops over which the sun of afternoon was extending long golden arms. They had been in every one of those thirteen little houses and had met with nothing but gaiety and kindness. They had not seen a sign of Old Bushara and his knife.

"He must live in a den somewhere," said Betsy.

"I wonder where," said Tacy, looking behind her.

"He must have been out peddling," said Tib. "That's what most of the Syrians do for a living. They go out with horses and buggies or take satchels on their backs."

Of course that was where he was!

"Oh well," said Tib, "we have votes enough already."

"Votes enough!" said Betsy. "If you're not queen, I'd like to know the reason why."

"Won't Julia and Katie be mad!" said Tacy.

They climbed triumphantly, thinking how mad Julia and Katie would be.

IX

THE QUARREL AGAIN

JULIA and Katie were mad all right.

It was now that the quarrel began to get so serious that all of them were sorry it had started. They wanted to end it, but they didn't know how. It was just as if the five of them were piled in a cart which was rattling down Hill Street lickety split, and no one could stop it. It was the worst quarrel they had ever had, and they never had another like it.

When Betsy, Tacy, and Tib came down the Big Hill, Julia and Katie were still sitting on the Rays' side lawn, working on their decorations. They had worked all day, just stopping for dinner. They were tired, but they looked happy.

They had decided not to have a Maypole since it wasn't May any more, but they were going to decorate one of the side lawn maples. They were going to twist it with green and pink streamers up to the lowest branch, and from there they were going to stretch ribbons and garlands to either side of the throne. Of course they were not putting up these decorations yet, for fear it might rain before the celebration, but they had them ready

Tired and triumphant, Betsy, Tacy and Tib came down through the orchard and kitchen garden. When they saw the beautiful streamers piled around Julia and Katie, they felt queer for a moment.

Tib said quickly, "We've got the most votes. Let's give in. I can wear my accordion-pleated dress and be a flower girl."

Tacy looked at Betsy, but Betsy got stubborn sometimes. And when Betsy got stubborn, Tacy was stubborn too because she didn't like to go back on Betsy.

"No, sir," Betsy said.

"We planned it first," said Tacy.

They walked down the side lawn where Julia and Katie were sitting.

"Lookee here, lookee here, lookee here," they cried, waving their petition.

Julia and Katie looked up and amazement spread over their faces. They could see at once that the petition had two pages. They could see that it was black with names.

"Where have you been?" asked Katie sharply.

"Don't you wish you knew!"

"There aren't *that* many Ekstroms up on the Big Hill," Julia cried.

Betsy, Tacy, and Tib danced about, acting exasperating.

But they couldn't resist telling where they had been, so in just a minute they shouted, "We've been to Little Syria, that's where!"

"You haven't!" cried Julia and Katie in dazed unbelief.

"How did you get there?"

"We walked there."

"But you're not allowed . . ."

"No one ever told us not to. And it's not on the other side of Lincoln Park either So don't say it is."

Julia and Katie did not try to say it was.

They looked at each other, and their great disappointment seemed to fill the air. But Katie spoke in a matter-of-fact tone.

"There's no need to fight. We'll count votes like we said we would. Where's our list, Julia?"

They got out the list and Betsy, Tacy, and Tib flung their list down beside it. Betsy, Tacy, and Tib knew that they had the most votes, but they didn't enjoy having them as much as they had expected.

Julia and Katie began grimly to read.

In a moment anger flared out like a flame from gray ashes.

"What's this?" cried Julia.

"What under the sun!" cried Katie. "You don't expect us to count this gibberish, I hope."

"What gibberish?" demanded Betsy.

"This!"

Julia and Katie pointed with trembling furious fingers to that writing which ran from right to left.

"It's all right," said Betsy. "It's Arabic."

"Arabic!" cried Julia and Katie.

"You might have just scrawled it yourselves for all we know," said Julia.

"You might have let a chicken run over the paper," said Katie.

"Well, we didn't!" said Betsy indignantly. "Every single one is a name."

"Every single one of what?" asked Julia.

When Betsy looked she wasn't sure herself. You couldn't tell where one word stopped and another began. Only Mr. Meecham's signature, and his daughter's, and his coachman's looked right.

"I know how you can count it," said Tib. "There were thirteen houses down there, and about ten people in a family . . ."

"As if we could count that way!" scoffed Katie.

"No, sir! You have to throw out these names that aren't in English."

"We won't!"

"You must!"

"We won't!"

"You've got to!"

"We won't!"

Their voices were so loud now that Margaret came scrambling up the terrace from the Riverses' lawn where she had been playing with the Rivers children. The Rivers children came too; and Paul and Freddie who had been playing on the Kellys' lawn; and Paul's dog and some other dogs and children.

The quarrel began to get bad. In a moment the Rays' side lawn looked as though a cyclone had struck it. Arms and legs were flying in all directions, and lists were flying, and pink and green streamers were flying. Margaret was shouting and Paul's dog was barking.

Mrs. Ray came to the kitchen door.

"What's this? What's this?" she asked.

"They won't count our Arabic votes!" cried Betsy, leaping frantically about.

"Your what?"

"Our Arabic votes that we got in Little Syria."

"In Little Syria!" said Mrs. Ray. Her tone was so astounded that Betsy, Tacy, and Tib shrank into silence. Tacy sniffed back her tears and looked at Betsy. Tib looked at Betsy too. After all, this was Betsy's mother, standing so tall and stern.

"Have you three been to Little Syria?" asked Mrs. Ray.

"Yes, ma'am," said Betsy.

"Who said you could go there?"

"Nobody. But nobody said we couldn't."

"Papa told you not to go beyond Lincoln Park."

"This isn't beyond Lincoln Park," said Betsy. "This is in the other direction."

Mrs. Ray looked nonplussed. But she was never nonplussed long. She spoke with vigor.

"Whether or not you did wrong to go to Little Syria can be decided later. But this quarreling must be stopped right now. Papa suggested a plan and you all agreed to it. You all agreed that the one who got the most votes should be queen. And you promised too that the losers would be good sports. So count your votes and let's decide the matter."

"But that's what we've been trying to do," cried Julia desperately.

"We can't read the names," said Katie. "Look at the writing, Mrs. Ray!"

She thrust the list with its strange scratchings into Mrs. Ray's hands.

"See?" said Julia. "They ought not to be allowed to count them."

"We will too count them!" shouted Betsy, Tacy, and Tib.

"You won't!"

"We will!"

"You won't!"

"We will!"

Julia burst out in a shaking voice, "Never mind! I wish I'd never thought about being a queen. Everything's spoiled! Everything! Everything!"

Her voice broke, and she bent to pick up streamers in order to conceal her quivering lips. She looked ready to cry, but Julia never cried, not even when she was spanked.

She didn't cry now, but Tib did. Tib cried good and hard.

"I wish I'd never thought about it too," wailed Tib.

Mrs. Ray knew how to be cross when children were naughty. But she wasn't cross now. She spoke gently.

"I won't try to settle this," she said. "It was papa's plan. And he'll be at his lodge meeting tonight and won't be home until late. You children come over in the morning and we'll straighten everything out. Julia, Betsy, it's time to clean up for supper."

Katie and Tacy went home, but they didn't go together. Katie stalked ahead, and Tacy went behind with her face in her sleeve. Tib ran down the hill and her tears ran faster than her feet. All the children and dogs went home.

Julia and Betsy went into the house, with Margaret following them. Margaret stared from one to the other with her round, black-lashed eyes. Margaret had never seen such a quarrel before. She was pretty surprised.

Betsy kept remembering how Julia had looked when she said, "Everything's spoiled! Everything! Everything!" Betsy didn't want to remember it. She couldn't help it.

She glanced guiltily toward Julia now, but Julia looked poised and icy. She had washed her face and combed her hair, and was reading a book. She didn't look at Betsy or speak to her. She acted as though Betsy weren't there.

Betsy washed her face and combed her hair too. She crossed her braids in back and tied the ribbons the best she could. (Usually Julia tied them.) She asked Margaret if she didn't want to play with blocks. And Margaret said she did. So Betsy made her a big block house and laughed and made jokes and looked at Julia now and then. But Julia did not look their way at all.

They had supper without their father, and that seemed odd. Julia talked to her mother in a cool grown-up way. Betsy talked to her too, and both of them talked to Margaret. But they didn't talk to each other.

When the games started in the street Julia didn't go outdoors. She kept on reading her book. Betsy went out, but the games weren't any fun. They weren't any fun at all that night.

"How's Katie?" asked Betsy. For Katie wasn't there. Neither was Tib.

"Bad," said Tacy. "She feels pretty bad."

"So does Julia," said Betsy. After a moment she said, "They ought to feel bad too. Not wanting to count our votes, after that long trip we took and everything."

"Um-hum," said Tacy. She sounded doubtful.

"I don't like to have Katie feel quite so bad though," she said. "She's pretty good to me sometimes."

"Julia's all right too," said Betsy.

She knew that Tacy was hoping she would say, "Let's give in." But she couldn't quite say it. Betsy was stubborn sometimes.

When she went into the house she glanced at Julia, but Julia didn't even look up. She kept on reading her book.

Their mother said it was bedtime and Julia and Betsy went upstairs. They undressed and put on their nightgowns in silence. They said their prayers and climbed into bed and lay there without speaking.

Mrs. Ray came upstairs to tuck them in. She always did. She sat down beside them, looking worried.

"In this family," she said, "we have a rule. We never go to sleep angry. Sometimes during the day we get angry and do wrong things and say things we don't mean. Everyone does. But before we go to sleep we always say we are sorry. We always make up. Always."

After a moment Julia said stiffly, "I'm sorry, Betsy."

"I'm sorry," Betsy answered.

They kissed each other.

Their mother looked closely into their faces. She didn't seem satisfied. Maybe she thought they hadn't sounded sorry; at least, not sorry enough. But presently she leaned down and kissed them, first Julia and then Betsy. She took the lamp and went downstairs.

"Good night," she called.

"Good night," called Julia and Betsy.

But they didn't go to sleep.

The street lamp at the corner made a glow on the sloping walls. Sweet summer smells came in the open window with the loving chirping of birds. Betsy felt terrible. She could not forget that look on Julia's face when she had said, "Everything's spoiled." First she would remember how happy Julia had looked with her pink and green streamers piled around her; and then she would remember her pale strained face when she said, "Everything's spoiled."

Betsy lay still and thought about Julia. She thought how proud she was of her when she sang, and played, and gave her recitations. Julia was different from all the other children. There was nobody like her.

She thought how good Julia was to her sometimes. How she tied her hair ribbons. How she helped her with arithmetic. How she never would let anybody pick on her.

"You leave my little sister alone!" Julia always said.

She thought of the fun they had together when they went out on family picnics. She and Julia always sat in the back seat of the surrey and played games. She thought what fun they had on vacations at Uncle Edward's farm. Even when Julia was playing with

Katie, and Betsy was playing with Tacy and Tib, they had fun. The quarrels had been fun up to now.

Betsy began to cry, but softly, so that Julia would not hear her. Julia on her side of the bed had not moved or stirred. Betsy was determined that Julia should not hear her cry. She cried too easily anyhow, and Julia never cried. Betsy pressed her fist against her mouth, but tears trickled down her cheeks and down her chin and even down her neck inside the collar of her nightgown.

Then from the other side of the bed she heard a sound. It was a sob, a perfectly gigantic sob.

"Betsy!" cried Julia, and she came rolling over and hugged Betsy tight. "I'm sorry."

"I'm sorry too," Betsy wept.

"I don't want to be queen," Julia sobbed. "I want Tib to be queen."

"But Tib doesn't want to be queen," wept Betsy. "And Tacy doesn't want her to be queen, if it makes you and Katie feel bad. I'm the mean one. I'm the stubborn one."

"I'm meaner than you are," said Julia. "I always was."

She cried so that her tears ran down Betsy's face. Their wet cheeks pressed together.

"I've been feeling terrible," said Julia, "about your going down to Little Syria. It was mean of us to go to that Ice Cream Social and get so many votes. Why, I'm your big sister. I'm supposed to take care of you. And here I practically drove you down to Little Syria. You might have been killed. That awful place. . . ."

Betsy sat bolt upright.

"Why, Julia!" she cried. "It isn't awful at all. It's a lovely place."

"What do you mean?" asked Julia, blowing her nose.

"I mean just what I say. The people gave us raisins and figs. They're lovely people."

Julia gave Betsy her handkerchief, and Betsy blew her nose too. They both stopped crying, and Betsy told Julia all about the trip to Little Syria.

They talked and talked, but in whispers for they weren't supposed to be talking. They were supposed to be asleep. Betsy told her about the hubble-bubble pipe, the red cap with a tassel, the kibbee, the goat. Julia was fascinated.

They talked so late that their father came home from his lodge meeting. They heard their mother talking with him; she was telling him about the quarrel. They heard their mother come upstairs to tuck in Margaret who slept in the back bedroom. She looked in on them too, but they pretended they were asleep. After that the house was very quiet.

"It's the latest we've ever been awake," said Julia.

"It's tomorrow, I imagine," Betsy said.

"I suppose," said Julia, "we'd better go to sleep."
And they kissed each other good night.

Julia rolled over, and Betsy tucked in cozily behind her. They didn't go to sleep right away, but they didn't talk any more.

Betsy felt happy, delicious, emptied of trouble. Only one small perplexity remained.

If Julia wouldn't be queen, and Tib wouldn't be queen, who would be queen?

"We just have to use those streamers," Betsy thought as she slipped through a gray mist into sleep.

X

A PRINCESS

IN THE morning they were happy. They smiled at each other as they washed and dressed. Julia tied Betsy's hair ribbons. Then she hurried down to the kitchen.

"Mamma," she said. "I want Tib to be queen. I really mean it. I've told Betsy so."

Betsy was close behind her.

"No, sir," she said. "Julia's going to be queen. Tacy and Tib and I are going to be flower girls."

Mrs. Ray was making coffee. She put the coffee pot down and put her arms around them; they had a big hug. Mr. Ray was shaving at the kitchen basin. He looked around, with his face covered with lather, and smiled broadly.

"Katie and Tacy and Tib are out on the hitching block," he said. "Go and ask them what they have to say about all this. Then bring them in here because *I* have something to say. I have plenty to say."

Betsy wondered whether it concerned Little Syria. And Julia, evidently, had the same thought.

"It really wasn't Betsy's fault about Little Syria, papa," she said. "Katie and I got so many votes at that Ice Cream Social that Betsy and Tacy and Tib just had to do something to catch up. And she says it's a very nice place. The people were lovely to them."

"Yes," said Mr. Ray, "I heard quite a lot about Little Syria yesterday. Mr. Meecham and his daughter came into the store to buy shoes."

"That's where they were coming from when we saw them!" Betsy thought. She wished her father would say more, but he didn't. Her mother spoke briskly.

"Run out to see what the children want," she said. "Then bring them in here, so papa can have his say."

Julia and Betsy ran out.

Katie was the first one off the hitching block.

"Julia," she said, "let's let Tib be queen. I sort of worried last night, thinking about those kids going down to Little Syria all alone."

Tib interrupted.

"But I've decided not to be queen," she said. "I want Julia to be queen."

"I'd just as soon let Julia be queen. Wouldn't you, Betsy?" asked Tacy.

"Yes, I would," said Betsy. "I was coming out to tell you."

"Well, I won't be!" said Julia. "I feel just as Katie does. I think Tib ought to be queen."

At the same moment all of them saw how funny it was to be talking that way, and they all began to laugh.

"Come in the house a minute," Julia said. "Papa has something he wants to say to us. But I warn you right now that I will *not* be queen."

"And neither will I," said Tib.

They marched into the kitchen where the coffee was bubbling, and Mrs. Ray was pouring glasses of milk and stirring oatmeal and turning sausage and making toast all at the same time. Mr. Ray had finished shaving. He had put on his collar and tie, and he looked nice. He was tying Margaret's napkin around her neck.

The five little girls came in, laughing.

"We're still fighting, papa," said Julia. "But now it's not about being queen. It's about not being queen."

"Well, for Pete's sake!" said Mr. Ray.

"You see," said Julia, "I won't be queen. . . ."

"And neither will I," said Tib.

"No matter how many votes I have," continued Julia. "And I'm sure I don't have enough."

"But we'll throw out the Arabic votes," said Betsy.

"No you won't!" said Julia. "Syrian votes are just as good as any other votes."

"Where are their wings?" asked Mrs. Ray gaily. "Feel for their wings, Margaret. They're white feathery things and they crop out near shoulders."

Margaret jumped up and started feeling for wings. Everyone started feeling for wings, and it tickled, and things grew lively.

"Let's have the coronation soon," said Mrs. Ray, "while we're feeling so happy."

"And while the weather's so fine," said Mr. Ray.

"No telling how long it will last," said Mrs. Ray.

"The fine weather?" asked Mr. Ray, winking at her.

Julia and Katie, Betsy, Tacy, and Tib were bewildered by this talk.

"But papa!" cried Julia, "how can we have a coronation without a queen?"

"That's what I have to talk to you about," said Mr. Ray. He sat down and crossed his legs and looked from one to another. "I heard something yesterday," he said, "that will interest you very much." He paused, then spoke impressively:

"There's a real princess in town."

"A real princess!" came an astonished chorus.

"A real princess," Mr. Ray repeated.

"Someone from the old country?" asked Tib.

"Someone from the old country."

"Is she of the blood royal?" asked Betsy.

"She's of the blood royal."

"Is she down at the Melborn Hotel?" asked Julia.

"No. She isn't. But she's here in Deep Valley. How would you like to go to see her and ask *her* to be queen?"

"Oh, we'd like it! We'd like it!" The kitchen resounded.

"Do you suppose she'll consent?" asked Julia.

"Where is she?" asked Katie.

"You never could guess, so I'll tell you. She's in Little Syria. Imagine," he said to Betsy, Tacy, and Tib, "having a princess right under your nose and not recognizing her!"

"Oh, I'm sure we didn't see her, papa," cried Betsy. And Tacy and Tib nodded vigorous agreement.

"Did you see the old man called Old Bushara?"

"No, we didn't. He was out peddling or something."

"Well, this girl is Old Bushara's granddaughter."

Old Bushara's granddaughter!

"And *she's* not away peddling, for Mr. Meecham saw her yesterday. Pour yourself some coffee, Jule," he said to Mrs. Ray, "and sit down while I'm telling the story.

"Mr. Meecham and I," he began, "started talking about his neighbors. He's interested in them, and no wonder. They come from a very interesting country. You can read about their country in the Bible. The Deep Valley Syrians are Christians, but most Syrians are Mohammedans. Syria is under the control of the Turks, and the Turks are Mohammedans too. A good many of the Christian Syrians are coming to America these days. And they come for much the same reason that our Pilgrim fathers came. They want to be free from oppression and religious persecution. We ought to honor them for it.

"Most of them come from the Lebanon district," Mr. Ray went on. "You've heard about Lebanon,

I'm sure. King Solomon's temple was built from the cedars of Lebanon. Cedars still grow on those wild Lebanon hills; and in the ravines and valleys some brave groups of people still keep their loyalty to their native Syrian princes . . . in spite of the Turks. Emeers, these princes are called, and their daughters and granddaughters are emeeras or princesses. This Old Bushara is an emeer of Lebanon, and his grand-daughter is an emeera."

"Mr. Ray," said Tib, "is that why Old Bushara gets so mad and chases boys when they yell 'dago' at him?"

"It probably is," said Mr. Ray. "An emeer of Lebanon is a very proud man, and he should be. He's an ancient prince of a very ancient race."

A dazzled silence filled the kitchen.

Mr. Ray looked from Betsy, to Tacy, to Tib.

"It was wrong of you to go to Little Syria yesterday without permission," he said. "But it's quite all right to go there *with* permission. If Mrs. Kelly and Mrs. Muller are willing, you and Julia and Katie may go there and ask Old Bushara's granddaughter to come and be your queen."

"Why don't you go today," suggested Mrs. Ray, "and have your coronation tomorrow?"

"Before the weather changes," put in Mr. Ray.

Mr. and Mrs. Ray smiled at each other.

148

Katie and Tacy and Tib ran home to breakfast, and they came back saying that they could go to Little Syria. So the five of them went that very afternoon.

Betsy, Tacy, and Tib led the way up the Big Hill. They stopped to invite Mrs. Ekstrom to the coronation.

"Kings and queens! Kings and queens!" said Mrs. Ekstrom, throwing up her hands.

"Oh, no, Mrs. Ekstrom," said Julia. "There isn't going to be a *king*."

"That's a wonder," Mrs. Ekstrom answered.

But she said she would come to the coronation. She wouldn't miss it, she said.

Betsy, Tacy, and Tib took Julia and Katie through the Secret Lane, and past the Mystery House, and down through a fold of the hill and up again. They stood hand in hand on the high rocky point looking down on their discovered valley. Betsy and Tacy and Tib pointed out and explained. Julia and Katie listened and asked questions. It was pleasant for Betsy and Tacy and Tib to know more than Julia and Katie knew, for once.

They went down the hill, running sometimes and walking sometimes, picking columbines and yellow bells and Jacks-in-the-pulpit and daisies to make a bouquet for the princess.

"I wonder why you didn't see her yesterday," said

Julia.

"I suppose," said Betsy, "they sort of keep a princess hidden."

"I wonder which house she's in," said Tacy.

"Let's go straight to Naifi's and ask," Tib suggested. "Her father speaks English, you know."

They had reached the path which ran down to the settlement and the thirteen little ramshackle houses came into view. Loud harsh talk rose from the vegetable gardens, but no one felt nervous.

"That's just the way Syrians talk," Betsy explained.

They did not go around behind Mr. Meecham's house today. They skipped straight down the little dusty street, calling "hello" right and left to the many friends they had there.

They heard someone playing a flute.

"That's a munjaira," Tacy said off-handedly.

"And Naifi's grandfather," said Tib, "will likely be smoking a hubble-bubble pipe."

As a matter of fact, he was, when they entered Naifi's house.

The little grandmother answered their knock; and they knew from her smiling hospitable motions that she was inviting them in. They came in, and there sat the grandfather, cross-legged, smoking his pipe.

He took the pipe out of his mouth and smiled at them. And the grandmother ran to the back door and called loudly. Naifi's father and Naifi came hurrying in from the garden.

"Today you are five," said Naifi's father merrily.

"Five," laughed Naifi.

"Five," chuckled the grandfather. He held five fingers up to the grandmother and pointed to the children and chuckled. She chuckled too.

Betsy introduced Julia and Katie.

"They are our sisters," she said. And the grandmother ran for the jars of raisins and figs. They all sat down on that low divan which ran around the room and ate raisins and figs.

Julia and Katie waited politely for Betsy or Tacy or Tib to state their errand. Tacy and Tib waited for Betsy. So after a moment Betsy said, "We came to ask you a question. Will you tell us, please, which is Bushara's house?"

"Bushara's house?" asked Naifi's father, looking startled.

"Where does Old Bushara live?" asked Tib.

"And his granddaughter?" added Tacy. Tacy was shy with people she didn't know very well. But she was so eager to find the princess that she forgot to be shy.

Naifi's father stared at them. He threw back his black head and laughed. He spoke rapidly in Syrian, and the grandfather, the grandmother, and Naifi all laughed too.

The visitors looked at one another in surprise. They could not imagine what had been said that was funny.

The old man stood up, tall in his red tasseled cap. He put his hand across his breast.

"Here, here is Bushara!" he said.

He flung his arms about.

"Bushara's house!" he cried.

He pointed to Naifi.

"Bushara's grand . . . daughter," he ended.

Julia and Katie, Betsy, Tacy, and Tib sat as if stunned.

Betsy, Tacy, and Tib turned timid faces toward Naifi. Naifi was the princess! Naifi with whom they had picnicked on the hill, Naifi with whom they had tramped from end to end of Little Syria, Naifi at whom rough boys had shouted "Dago!"

Seeing her sister struck dumb with amazement, Julia told Naifi's father why they had come. She talked prettily, just as though she were reciting. She told him that they had heard about the Syrian emeera; she told him that they were crowning a Queen of Summer tomorrow and wanted Naifi to be queen.

"We will come to get her, and my father will drive her home. Mr. Meecham can tell you all about us.

We do hope she can come."

Julia talked so nicely that the children were surprised to see Naifi's father's merry face grow dark.

Naifi looked anxiously from the strange little girl to her father. She did not understand very much of what was being said, but she could see that her father did not like it. She listened attentively as he spoke in an earnest voice.

"It is true," he said, "that my father was an emeer of Lebanon. And that is an honor for which respect is due him, more respect than he receives sometimes, perhaps. But he is also an American. He is trying to get the citizenship and so am I. And that will be a greater honor, to be Americans.

"No, no," he continued, shaking his head, "I do not want my Naifi to play the Syrian emeera. She is forgetting about such things. She is an American now. Are you not, my heart, my eyes?"

Naifi nodded until her braids swung up and down. She stood very straight, and her eyes were bright.

"American!" she said.

"American!" said the Emeer of Lebanon, striking his breast again.

"American!" said his wife. For even the old grandmother knew the word "American."

Something in the way they said "American" gave Betsy an idea. She jumped from her seat.

"Of course," she cried. "But this is to be an American celebration. It's an American queen we want Naifi to be."

"It is?" asked Naifi's father, looking puzzled.

Tacy followed Betsy's lead like lightning.

"We're going to have a big flag up, red, white, and blue, Mr. Bushara," she said.

Julia and Katie fell into line.

"I'm going to sing 'The Star Spangled Banner,'" said Julia. "And Katie maybe is going to recite Lincoln's Gettysburg Address."

"It's almost the Fourth of July, you know," Katie put in.

Tib looked from one to another in surprise. "When did you plan all this?" she began. But Betsy kicked her.

"It's lovely," Tib said hastily.

Naifi's father translated all they had said. He and his family talked in Syrian excitedly, waving their arms. Smiles broke over their faces, and Naifi's father put his hand on Naifi's head.

"She may go," he said. "I will bring her myself. I start tomorrow on a trip with my horse and buggy selling the linens and laces. But first I will bring her to your house, to be your American queen."

So it was decided! And Julia and Katie, Betsy, Tacy, and Tib were enormously elated. They didn't stay much longer. There was too much to be done on Hill Street for the morrow's celebration. But of course Julia and Katie took time to call on the goat.

The grandmother, meanwhile, was whispering to the grandfather, and giving him little nudges. Naifi started whispering to him too, and at last he rose as though offended and went into a room and shut the door.

Just as the visitors were ready to leave, he reappeared.

He had changed his garments and wore long flowing robes gathered slightly at the ankles. His red fez

was wound with folds of white which hung down to his shoulders, framing his brown seamed face. His manner was grave, his bearing was majestic. The children knew without being told that this was his garb of an emeer.

"It's wonderful, Mr. Bushara," said Julia. "Thank you for putting it on."

"Thank you," murmured the others, gazing with shining eyes.

Betsy whispered to Julia.

"Maybe," said Julia quickly, "Naifi could wear her emeera clothes tomorrow?"

Naifi's father smiled. He did not answer.

The old man was not listening. He was looking up at the hills, those green gentle slopes which rose around the valley in which he had found a new home.

"Those hills," he said haltingly, "they not the hills of Lebanon. And Bushara, not an emeer of Lebanon. Not now. Not any longer. Bushara, an American now."

Julia and Katie, Betsy, Tacy, and Tib said good-by and started toward home. After they had climbed a while without speaking, Julia said soberly, "They think a lot of being Americans; don't they?"

"They certainly do," Katie answered.

"Boys like Sam ought to know more about them," said Tib. Tib sometimes said very sensible things.

"Let's give Naifi a fine celebration," said Betsy.

"A real American celebration," said Tacy, and everyone agreed.

All the way home they made plans for crowning an American queen.

XI

A QUEEN

N AIFI was crowned queen next day.

She was crowned on the Rays' side lawn under one of the two young maples which Betsy's father had set out; it was just the right size.

Pink and green streamers were wound around the tree up to the lowest branch, and from that point chains of flowers ran to either side of Mr. Ray's armchair. It was a big leather armchair. It made a fine throne.

A large American flag overhung all, and small American flags were stuck into the ground in a half circle behind the throne. Flags which were ordinarily stored away in closets and brought out only on patriotic holidays had been produced by dozens to make Naifi's coronation strictly American.

Paul and Freddie borrowed flags all up and down Hill Street while Margaret and Hobbie and the Rivers children picked flowers on the hill and Betsy and Tacy and Tib wove garlands and Julia and Katie decorated. Everything was done without the smallest disagreement. Everyone was kind to everyone else. And the mothers were so pleased that Mrs. Ray made lemonade, and Mrs. Kelly baked a cake, and Matilda baked cookies. Even a coronation needs refreshments.

When the decorating was finished, the children went out to invite people. Julia and Katie, Betsy, Tacy, and Tib skipped down to Pleasant Street to tell Dorothy and Alice what time to come. All the neighbors were invited, and many of them came. By half past two o'clock the lawn was full of people.

Mrs. Ekstrom came all the way down the Big Hill. And Mrs. Benson came, and Mrs. Rivers and the children. Mrs. Hunt who was deaf and dumb came, bringing her crowing baby. Mrs. Granger came, and Miss Williams, and Ben, and the boy named Tom.

Julia and Betsy and Margaret and Katie and Tacy all wore their best Sunday dresses. When they stood together they made a bouquet of light summer tints. Tib wore the accordion-pleated dress. Dorothy, who had dark curls, wore a red dress; it was silk. And Alice's dress was blue, of thin nun's veiling.

Grown-ups sat on the lawn in chairs but the children kept racing to the Rays' front steps to look down Hill Street. They were pretty worked up about a princess coming. At last they saw an unfamiliar horse, a buggy loaded with satchels. It was Mr. Bushara, bringing Naifi.

He stopped at the hitching block and jumped out and pulled off his hat. The sun shone on his glistening cap of hair. He lifted Naifi out of the buggy, and his face was as proud as it was merry.

"Look at that, my heart!" he said, pointing to the big American flag.

The children swooped down upon them.

Naifi was a princess out of the Arabian Nights. Betsy could not have invented one more lovely. A cloud of chiffon floated about her face. Her mouth was hidden, but her dark eyes were sparkling. They were rimmed with sooty black.

Her dress was long and full-skirted, like the one she

had worn the day they saw her first. But this one was of soft rich cashmere, purple in color and embroidered in gold. The short jacket was gold-embroidered too. Bloomers were tied at her ankles above little slippers of gold.

She was laden with jewelry . . . bracelets, rings, ear-rings. . . .

"Naifi! You're wonderful! You're beautiful!" cried the children.

"Hel-lo," said Naifi. "Hel-lo, hel-lo, hel-lo."

Mrs. Ray asked her father to stay, but he said that he had to go. He returned to his buggy and drove down Hill Street with a proud smiling face.

The children hurried Naifi into the Rays' parlor. There the parade assembled. Mrs. Ray was going to play the piano for it; Tom was going to play the violin.

On the lawn the other mothers and the guests waited expectantly. The sun shone down, and the air smelled of roses.

"No more queens, I hope," Mrs. Muller said to Mrs. Kelly.

"It will be something else next week," Mrs. Kelly answered.

Mrs. Ray played a rousing march. It was named "Pomp and Circumstance." She played it with spirit and Tom played it with her on his violin. The proces-

sion streamed out of the door to the porch, down the porch steps, and over the lawn.

First came Margaret and Hobbie waving flags. They waved them in time to the music.

Next came Paul and Freddie in their best suits. They were pages. Pages walked straight and tried not to smile.

Then came Betsy and Tacy, Tib and Alice. They scattered flowers as gracefully as they knew how. They scattered the flowers picked that morning on the hill, columbines and daisies and the scarlet Indian paintbrush.

Treading on the flowers came Naifi, dimples flashing. And just behind walked Dorothy, holding the edge of Naifi's dress. Julia and Katie came last of all, bearing a pillow with a crown upon it.

Betsy's mother played three or four crashing chords. Naifi seated herself on the throne. Two of the royal party darted indoors. The rest seated themselves on the grass.

Dorothy rose and swept her brown curls almost to the ground in a curtsey.

"Your majesty," she said in her sweet voice, "we will now endeavor to entertain you."

Mrs. Ray began to play the Baby Dance. Tib jumped up, picked her skirt up by the edges and made a pirouette.

After the Baby Dance, which was loudly applauded, two black cats capered out on the lawn. Mrs. Ray played the Cat Duet and Betsy and Tacy sang it. They were loudly applauded too.

Katie recited the Gettysburg Address. She despised reciting but she was too patriotic to refuse. When she had finished, she and Julia knelt before the Queen. They held the cushion high and Dorothy lifted the crown.

As she put it on Naifi's head, Mrs. Ray, inside the house, began to play "Hearts and Flowers."

Julia went up and stood on the porch steps, looking solemn. Paul and Freddie handed out flags. Mrs. Ray switched to "The Star Spangled Banner." Everyone stood up, of course, and Julia sang.

She sang as only Julia could. Betsy thought about George Washington. She thought about Abraham Lincoln. She thought about Theodore Roosevelt, the President. She thought about Old Bushara saying that he was an American now.

At the end of a verse Julia smiled suddenly and asked everyone to sing. Everyone sang "The Star Spangled Banner" and waved flags. Naifi's eyes were something to watch then. Bright as diamonds, they looked about the lawn at the tossing banners.

After that it was just a party with plenty of lemonade, cookies, and cake.

In the midst of all the gaiety no one noticed Mr. Goode, the postman. He had trudged up Hill Street on his usual afternoon round and arrived at the Rays' front steps. He paused to look around, holding a letter in his hand.

"Hey, there!" he said to Mrs. Ray who was passing a tray full of glasses.

She stopped and came toward him.

"Hello, Mr. Goode. Won't you have some lemon-ade?"

"Don't care if I do," he said. He slipped off his bag to rest his shoulder, but still he held the letter in his hand.

"Something for us?" asked Mrs. Ray.

"For Betsy and Tacy and Tib."

"All three of them?"

"All three of them. And if you ask me," he said, "it's pretty important." He handed it to her.

The envelope was large and square. It bore an un-familiar stamp. Turning it over, Mrs. Ray saw an official-looking seal.

"Betsy! Tacy! Tib! Come here!" she said. And Betsy, Tacy, and Tib came running, for there was something compelling in her voice. Other children crowded behind them, grown-ups too.

"It's a letter from Spain," said Mr. Goode. "Do you know anybody in Spain?"

Betsy and Tacy and Tib felt for one another's hands. They didn't speak for a moment.

Tib whispered desperately to Betsy, "What shall I do if he wants to marry me? I don't want to marry him. I want to be an American like Naifi."

Tacy whispered to Betsy too. "Do you suppose it's against the law to write to a king?"

Mrs. Ray noticed the whispers, the frightened faces.

"Do you want me to open it?" she asked. "I can't imagine what it can be, but it's certainly nothing to be afraid of."

Betsy swallowed a burr in her throat.

"Yes. Open it," she said.

She knew that Julia and Katie were there; she could see their curious faces. There was a crowd of people, and teasing could be very hard. But this was serious. If it was against the law to write to kings and they were going to be sent to jail, their mothers might as well know it. Their fathers would have to get them out.

Betsy and Tacy and Tib waited in frozen panic.

Mrs. Ray opened the envelope. She unfolded a rich creamy paper.

"Heavens and earth!" she said. And then, "Children! Children!"

Betsy and Tacy and Tib did not speak. They squeezed one another's hands.

"What did you do?" demanded Betsy's mother.

They did not answer.

"This letter," said Mrs. Ray, "comes from the King of Spain. At least it comes from his Palace. It seems to be written by a secretary. I can't pronounce his name."

"What does he say?" asked Tib in a trembling voice.

"He says that His Majesty thanks you for the sentiments expressed in your letter."

"Is that all?"

"That's all. Isn't it enough?"

It was quite enough.

With a common impulse Betsy, Tacy, and Tib flung their arms about each other. They jumped up and down shouting in a glad release from fear.

"How did you happen to write to him?" asked three mothers at once.

"Oh," said Betsy vaguely. "It was his birthday."

Tacy remembered something.

"But how did our letter get mailed?"

"That's so," said Tib. "We lost it."

They looked around the agitated circle. One face stood out above all others. It was red from suppressed laughter.

"On the hill you lost it," Mrs. Ekstrom said.

Mrs. Ekstrom had mailed it!

The letter passed from hand to hand. And Betsy, Tacy, and Tib felt mighty proud now that they knew they hadn't done anything wrong or stepped into trouble.

Getting a letter from a king was a perfect ending to an afternoon in which a queen was crowned.

The fathers came home in time for some remnants of cake and to see Naifi's regal costume. Betsy's father took Naifi home. She left with many smiles and nods of thanks. Everyone went home . . . the grown-ups, the children . . . except Tacy and Tib. They sat on the hitching block with Betsy in the long golden rays of the sun.

"I was scared when that letter came," said Tib.

"So was I," said Tacy. "I'm certainly glad none of us had to marry him."

"So am I," said Betsy. She thought about Old Bushara. "Why I wouldn't not be an American for a million dollars."

"Neither would I," said Tacy. "Not for ten million."

"Neither would I," said Tib. "I should say not!"

"It was fun," said Betsy, "playing kings and queens like this. But I don't think we'll do it any more."

"What will we do?" asked Tib.

"Oh, American things. Patriotic things."

Betsy had an idea.

"I'll tell you what we'll do," she said. "We'll write to Ethel Roosevelt."

Ethel Roosevelt was the President's daughter. She was just their age.

"We'll offer to come and see her in the White House," Tacy cried.

"I could dance my Baby Dance," said Tib.

"We could sing the Cat Duet," said Betsy. "We'll write the first thing in the morning."

And they did. But if Ethel Roosevelt ever received their letter, which is doubtful, she never got around to answering it. And so the plan to dance and sing in the White House came to nothing.

It didn't matter though. Betsy and Tacy and Tib found plenty of things to do. They soon stopped being ten years old. But whatever age they were seemed to be exactly the right age for having fun.